PRAISE FOR *WE WERE NOT KINGS*

"A deeply moving novel that fearlessly explores the complexities of brotherhood, masculinity, colourism, and what it takes to carve out a good life despite the traumas that follow you. Robert de la Chevotière's writing is luminous and devastatingly magnetic, a mark of a brilliant storyteller we should all keep our eyes on."

—Mai Nguyen, *New York Times* bestselling author of *Sunshine Nails*

WE WERE NOT KINGS

WE WERE NOT KINGS

A Novel

Robert de la Chevotière

Little a

This is a work of fiction. Names, characters, organizations, places, events, and incidents are either products of the author's imagination or are used fictitiously. Otherwise, any resemblance to actual persons, living or dead, is purely coincidental.

Published by Little A, New York

www.apub.com

EU product safety contact:
Amazon Media EU S. à r.l.
38, avenue John F. Kennedy, L-1855 Luxembourg
amazonpublishing-gpsr@amazon.com

ISBN-13: 9781662529351 (paperback)
ISBN-13: 9781662529368 (digital)

Cover design by Philip Pascuzzo
Cover image: © vectoraty / Adobe Stock; © Parrot Ivan, © majivecka / Shutterstock

Printed in the United States of America

To my children, Matthieu, Adora, and Mandela, may you wear your youth like your brown skin, may it always reflect the grace within. To my mother, Marvlyn, for teaching me what it is to have immeasurable courage. And to my cousin Babou, whose memory inspired this novel. Toujou en tchè en nou.

PART I

Chapter 1

Pointe-à-Pitre, July 1993

The heat stuck at the back of our throats like gravel in wet sand. June was so dry, you could say the devil himself walked among us. And when we prayed for the rain, we forgot we would have to deal with the mud, for when it fell that July, the deluge was constant. My grandmother said it was our ancestors crying for us, the pain of what they saw just too much for them to bear. Shortly before leaving for church, I caught her looking out the window. She stared blankly, and when she came to, she said, "The last time I saw rain like this, it wasn't just the ancestors who cried. I cried too. We all did." There was melancholy in her voice, a pain under her tongue. I felt it resurface when she, thinking of her deceased parents, looked up at the sky and said softly, "*Oh, Gilbert et Angéline, pléré, pléré.* Cry, cry."

The church sweltered inside. It felt like how it did in June, like hell runneth over, as if the Soufrière had erupted, and instead of the monsoon cooling the earth and healing the dry cracks in the dirt, we swam in lava, sweat drowning our fevered carcasses, my own body near convulsion to a sermon already much longer than necessary. Listening to Pastor Bishara preach about the prodigal son was a papaya whose flesh I had to painstakingly deseed by hand. Every time he opened his mouth, it burned me, as if someone smeared the leaf of the zouti plant across my face. I could hear nothing about the prodigal son, as this here son was already gone and had no intention of coming back. My grandmother looked over and, though seeing my obvious discomfort, still proceeded to cut her eyes at me. My brother smirked in his seat at my grandmother's gesture, while my mother, hypnotised by Pastor Bishara's words, remained oblivious to anything happening next to her in the pew.

"Listen to what Pastor is saying," whispered my grandmother as she leaned over my brother and pulled on my sleeve. "This sermon is for you."

I had lost all interest, more concerned with the rain and why the ancestors were crying, and whether they were upset with me. I looked over to the other side of the church and saw Magalie with her mother and brother. She saw me but didn't acknowledge me and fixed her gaze back on her father, Pastor Bishara. I felt such a resistance to the parable that I couldn't even hear it, not for a second. Maybe there would be a crack in the ceiling and the rain would pour through and force the service to stop. Or maybe God, hearing the blasphemy of my thoughts, would smite me where I sat. I would have preferred either of those than what Pastor Bishara did instead.

"Magalie Bishara," he said, calling out his daughter's name. I looked up to see her ushered towards him. And then he called mine. "Salomon Destin."

My heart dropped. I too was ushered forward by the congregation. As we stood next to him, he held our hands. From where I stood, I saw Magalie's mother, adjusting herself in the pew as she looked me up and down in silent vociferation of her disdain for me breathing the same air she did. She hated that her daughter and I were close friends.

"We need to bless these young people," said Pastor Bishara. "They both passed their final examinations. We know that so many of our youth don't get this far. We know it's not because of their ability that they aren't successful. We've all been through school, and we all know what it's like. As we congratulate these two, we also need to offer them our blessings."

To my chagrin he paused to look around at the congregation, smiling, as if he were looking in admiration at his own reflection. I stood there in all pretentiousness, trying to look calm while my spirit was throat deep choking on marbles. I didn't want to be at church, let alone stand at the podium with Pastor Bishara. He sweat profusely, his shirt and undershirt sticking to him like a wet suit, his arm hair thick and black and curled like mangled fishing line, rubbing against me, his large hand over mine, moist with his perspiration. And when he let go of my right hand, he put his hand on my shoulder, my back, my other shoulder, he moved to the back of us, of me, of Magalie, grabbed my other hand, smiled. It was a public molestation, and I wanted to be rescued. I no longer wished to hear him or smell his stale breath or feel his barbed-wire forearms. I tasted my own sweat as beads ran down my face and onto my lips. The thought that I was tasting his, mixed with mine, disgusted me.

"I want each and every one in this room to reach out your arms to these two. I want you to offer them your blessing . . . doesn't matter if you can't touch them . . . doesn't matter if you're in the back of the room," he said.

There were hands everywhere. Magalie and I had become food for a hungry horde of churchgoing zombies trying to get to us.

"We're seeing so many more of our young leave the island and head to the Continent. I am urging the two of you," he said to Magalie and me, "to go ahead and explore the world, but remember where you're from. Remember home. Remember you have a responsibility to come home and be home. Like the parable of the prodigal son, our arms will always be open wide for you, but don't be like the prodigal son. Don't wait until you're broken and have nothing before you return home. Come back sooner. Build your country. Be examples to those younger than you. Don't come home solely to bury your kin."

Pastor Bishara then prayed for us. My mother beamed with pride. Magalie's mother was equally as proud. Her older son, Clément, had finished school a few years before and was working in a government office in Basse-Terre, our island capital of Guadeloupe. She was happy that her daughter too had a chance to make something of herself. She was the most proud of all the mothers, in all of motherhood kingdom. Her children both exceeded expectations.

"I'll meet up with you later," I quietly said to Magalie as we exited the church.

"You're crazy if you think I'm meeting up with you in this rain," she replied.

"I'll bring the car."

"Boy, my mother is not letting me jump in no car with you after dark . . . or anytime," she said.

I felt a sudden shove on the shoulder as her mother forced her way between us, grabbing her daughter by the arm and rushing towards their vehicle, discreetly scolding her. Even at eighteen years old, Magalie was under her mother's watchful eye. Our rendezvous were always in secret, under the cover of a half-lit moon, or sometimes, at my house, in tandem with the lonely flickering lightbulb in the bedroom I shared with my brother. If her mother only knew how often she and I met at the elementary school, and that she visited my house when my parents and grandmother were out, and that we touched and kissed and superimposed our near naked bodies against her ignorance of our deviance, she would castrate me and never let Magalie out of her sight again.

Mrs. Bishara was a woman whose hateful ways were cloaked in the cloth. On Sundays, she was an usher in her husband's church. If she wasn't shouting "Amen" or "Hallelujah" while he preached, she was singing "How Great Thou Art" as she walked down the aisle with the collection plate. She never looked at anybody as she passed the plate between pews.

"Don't mind that woman," my grandmother would say, "acting like she's only got eyes for Jesus. Mary Magdalene had eyes for Jesus too."

To those of us who knew Mrs. Bishara outside of church, we knew that on the other days of the week, she did the devil's work. She never quite liked me, and in truth, she had a right not to like the boy who was sleeping with her daughter. My mother warned me about Mrs. Bishara, that I should leave her daughter alone, that I shouldn't make a mess I couldn't get myself out of. She felt strongly that Colette Bishara was not a Christian—not the generous, forgiving, nonjudgemental, loving Christian anyway.

The way I saw it, Colette Bishara was of that generation that believed she was inferior to white people, that her skin was ugly and worthless and a curse to the earth. It's hard to blame her, as likely this was passed down from her own mother, and life circumstances for dark-skinned Black women were less than ideal. Her marriage to Pastor Bishara was not surprising. Having a Black father and a Syrian mother, he had a light complexion, as did their children, Magalie and Clément. At the same time, I couldn't have pity on her. Self-loathing was one thing, but when manifested outwardly towards me, in particular with regards to her daughter, I couldn't feel anything about her circumstances or her sense of inferiority. To Colette Bishara, her children's complexion was a currency, a sort of legal tender that I could not afford. Boys like me would never be good enough for her daughter. It was the sort of thing that made my mother refer to her as a bloody hypocrite—a wolf in sheep's clothing. My grandmother often echoed my mother's sentiment. She also warned me: *"Lésé ti-moun à madam-là-sa."* Leave that woman's child alone.

"I feel it's just a matter of time until we're caught," said Magalie as she sat next to me on a bench in the school alcove that evening, safe from peering eyes, the rain having decided to hold off.

"There are worse things we could get caught for," I replied.

"I'm serious. What if someone came and saw us?"

The school was one of a few places that allowed us to be clandestine lovers in the dark. Getting caught in such a compromising situation wouldn't have been good, but it didn't matter much at that point. Soon, we would both leave for France. We'd be in different cities and wouldn't even see each other. Even that night, I wasn't really there. I was miles away, as absent as could be. She noticed.

"Are you still worried about your brother?" she asked. "Junior will be fine."

Maybe he would be fine, but I noticed the change in him. In all the ways we were different, he still looked up to me. And it wasn't only about me leaving, but him staying. There would be no buffer between him and our father. He would have our grandmother, but she was more coal to the fire than water. And when I mentioned Junior and my father in the same breath, Magalie paused and drew her own.

"Maybe that's just what they need, for you not to be there," she said with a heavy sigh.

But when our eyes met, she caught herself, realising the words that had come out of her mouth were nothing short of a faux pas. My father, as a topic of conversation, had become a sore spot for me. In all the ways that he was an alleged philanderer, he was still my father. And the rum had gotten a hold of him lately and had changed him in ways that a family man should never be changed. And my mother, despite all the hearsay, loved him. She loved him in a way that blinded her when it came to how he was with Junior—at least in a way that allowed her to make excuses for him.

"Junior will be OK. They all will," said Magalie, rubbing my back. "Remember, too much empathy gives people heartburn. The only heartburn I want you to have is for me."

"Yeah, in the dark school alcove with all our dark secrets," I said.

We laughed, but with hesitation on our smiles. It started to drizzle lightly. I looked up at the dark sky and thought back on my grandmother, entranced by the rain earlier that morning. Whatever it was for her, whatever pain seemed to resurface, at that moment for me, it was a resurgent, emotional lull.

Chapter 2

When I walked into the house that night, my mother immediately questioned me.

"Where are you coming from?"

"Mom," I said, dragging out the word. "I'm eighteen. It's seven o'clock on a Sunday night. Really?"

"Yes, really," she answered, cocking her head back. "And trust me, I know how old you are. I pushed your big ol' head out of me. Eighteen years later I still feel it. So yes, *really*, I can still ask you where you were."

In the background I could hear our neighbour, Mr. Jean, beat his gwo ka—his big drum, made of wood and hide, as was his nightly ritual. Although my generation amused ourselves with gwo ka beats, it was never something we embraced for its traditional values. It was like eating saltfish and boiled green bananas—we ate it because our mothers cooked it. But as we got older, nothing tasted better than a plate of boiled green banana and saltfish in a sauce of coconut milk. We enjoyed gwo ka and appreciated the various rhythms: the Toumblack, the Graj, the Mennde, the Padjambel, the Kalandja, the Woulé, and the Lewoz. Mr. Jean played his gwo ka, a sound I learned to love as much as I would eventually miss it. He kept on drumming well into the night.

"It's not him you should be asking questions," shouted my grandmother from the other room.

"Were you with that girl again tonight?" my mother asked, ignoring my grandmother's outburst.

"Yes."

"How many times do I have to tell you about that girl? I don't know why you don't listen to me."

"Let the boy be, Widelene," shouted my grandmother again. "The one you should be grilling, you never grill him."

"Sit down," my mother said to me, still ignoring my grandmother.

We sat at the table, joining my brother, who was already there having more servings of our Sunday dinner. I was expecting another lecture about Magalie. My mother was quiet at first. She looked at me, finding the words to speak.

"That was nice of Pastor Bishara today, to recognise the two of you."

I nodded in agreement.

"Did you like the sermon this morning?" she asked.

"Nope."

"Nope? What, did Magalie suck out your tongue?" she asked, unimpressed.

My brother chuckled.

"It was way too long."

"Do you agree with what he said?"

"I suppose. It makes sense," I replied.

"You don't have to do that, you know. Don't feel that you owe anyone in this house anything beyond the reasonable. You live your life for yourself."

"Don't you tell the boy such nonsense!" piped in my grandmother.

She made her way towards us and sat at the table. Never one to shy away from inserting herself in other people's conversations, my mother's conversation was now hers. To her, conversations were words which needed ears and tongues to give them any value. Conversations were like the wind. One never needed permission to bathe in it.

"I want to see my grandchild in my old age, not just when I'm on my deathbed or dead. I don't want to see him again just when he comes to bury me," she said.

"The dead don't see, Mom," said my mother.

"Oh, I will see. I will be lying in my coffin eyes wide open, watching you all come tell stories about me, listening to all your lies."

"Who said they will be lies? We will tell the truth. We might just shock you," said my mother.

My grandmother sucked her teeth. Then looking at my brother, scolded him. "You eating again, boy?"

"Pastor Bishara and his wife want their children to stay close to them," my mother said. "Myself, I want Magalie to go away and not come back. That little girl needs to spread her wings and not be stuck under her mother the same way her brother is. That woman made that boy stupid, a grown man like him acting like a damn child—a big old *tèbè*."

"That boy has a responsibility to be here," said my grandmother.

"What responsibility?" asked my mother.

"To his community. When your father and I brought you and your sister here from Haiti, we did that for you."

"It wasn't just about me and Mirlande. You left Haiti for you too. You have been here for years. We didn't stop you from going back."

"If we could have gone back, we would have. Do you know the amount of shame and guilt I feel when I go home after so many years, just to bury my family? So many faces I hardly recognise. Friends and family with children I don't even know."

"I can't imagine what that feels like, but that was still your choice."

"Maybe you're right. Maybe it was my choice. But you're also right when you say that you can't imagine it. It was hard leaving my home. I want to hate myself for not doing things differently. Don't teach him to leave. Teach him to honour the past. Honour us. He should honour you. Honour your father."

"He has a father too, you know," said my mother.

My grandmother again sucked her teeth, dismissing my mother's comment about my father. Then looking at my brother, she said, "If your belly had hands, it would slap you."

"Where is Fritzner?" my mother asked out loud to herself, in reference to my father, looking at her watch and then towards the door.

"What do you mean, where is Fritzner?" my grandmother asked, annoyed. "Where do you think he is?"

"Mom, don't start this nonsense again, please."

"You know where your husband is. I don't know why you want to act like you don't know."

"Mom, stop! I already asked you to leave him alone. Just mind your business."

"All right," my grandmother said. "I'm stopping, I'm stopping." She put her hands up in the air. "I'm not saying anything else. I will mind my business. Carry on with your child."

My grandmother had gotten tired of my father. My mother never spoke ill of him, but deep down she knew where he was. We all did.

"Salomon," my mother said to me, returning to her initial conversation after my grandmother's outbursts. "You have one life to live. I don't want you to suffocate on this island. And you don't want to hear this, but I don't want no girl to trap you, especially this one for Colette Bishara. You need to live. Just know that one day you will have to make space for your brother. You know he will follow in your footsteps. Be ready for him."

My grandmother listened, shaking her head. My brother put his fork down and sighed. Perhaps he was full, or just tired of listening to my mother. He was a few years younger than I was. Between the two of us, he was the more outgoing. He was funnier and had an uncanny sense of street smarts. He was the kind of person who, at their core, was a survivor. But he had to be. In infancy he was diagnosed with juvenile diabetes, so he's had to survive his entire childhood. In truth, we were very different people. I always felt he was smarter than I was. He grasped things faster and easier. He had a special kind of brilliance that never shone to those who didn't want to see it. His teachers saw him as inattentive, often expressing shock when he did well, often scolding him for how much better he could have done. I don't think he ever knew his brilliance, never being told it or shown it.

I remember the time he asked me about Camus's *The Stranger*, my class novel he'd picked up off the bedroom floor that we shared.

"Did Meursault shoot the Arab on the beach four times or five?" he had asked.

Clearly, the protagonist shot the knifed man on the beach five times. There was no disputing that. But my brother had understood something more.

"Yes, there were five shots fired, but did he really shoot him five times?" he asked.

I saw his brilliance as he went on to explain that the first shot didn't really count, even if it was all that was needed to kill the man on the beach. To my brother, that was the most unintentional shot. It was the succession of the other four that showed Meursault's intent. It was actually then that he wished the man dead. "Four more shots. Bap. Bab. Bab. Bap," I remember him saying as he mimicked shooting a pistol with his hand.

But there was another side to him, a more rebellious side, a side that was more carefree, one that didn't really consider others' perception of him or his life. These things provoked my father, and my father being short on patience had no time for him. He was the only person who called my brother by his actual name. Everyone called my brother "Junior," as he would dance to Bob Marley's music as a toddler. Where the iconic legend was known as "Tuff Gong," my brother became "Junior Gong," eventually only retaining the Junior. But to my father, he was Samuel—always Samuel. Sometimes, Junior's presence alone provoked my father, which made me wonder if he even liked his own son. The shame of it all is that they looked so much alike. Even at Junior's young age, one could tell that he would grow into my father's build. He had a thickness burgeoning out of him, his hands, shadows of large paws waiting to fill their potential.

I wish I had told him how brilliant he was, how special, how rare. In the age of kings—benevolent, mad, or wanting—Junior was the most aggrieved. Had I said something to him, perhaps his life would have turned out differently. Perhaps he would still be here.

Junior just sat there, listening to my mother talk to me, his empty plate in front of him. A short while later, my father entered the house. His intimidating frame meant nothing to my grandmother, who wasted no time starting in on him.

"Who sprayed Baygon? I see cockroach come out of hiding."

"So much for all that Sunday praise this morning, huh, Jesula," my father answered.

"Pastor Bishara missed you in church today. He was asking about you," she said.

"Let him ask," he replied, dismissing her.

"God is forgiving, you know. Even the most deceitful of men is forgiven."

"Mom, stop it!" interjected my mother.

"Jesula, I come in peace. Now I will go wash myself in peace and go to my bed in peace. Some of us have to work tomorrow," he said as he strolled past us.

"You call that work? Sitting in a rum distillery all day, drinking more than you make. I'm surprised the old *béké* hasn't fired you yet," said my grandmother.

"Thank God he hasn't, Jesula. Thank God you can still eat," he replied.

My mother, again, told my grandmother to stop and instructed my father to go along and wash himself.

"That's right. Just go bathe. Go wash her stink off you," said my grandmother.

My father stopped and looked hard at my grandmother. All of us in the room clearly understood her insinuation.

"What?" she asked, breaking the silence. "You need to be shamed. Men like you have no shame. What are you teaching these boys?"

"Mom, you need to stop," stressed my mother, visibly angry.

"Widelene," said my grandmother, looking my mother fiercely in the eyes. "Aren't you tired? Is this the disrespect you want from your husband? This nonsense from Fritzner is shameful. He eats Sunday dinner at your table and then goes out to see her for dessert!"

"You're doing this right here, right now?" my mother asked, embarrassed.

My mother was used to my grandmother interfering in her business, but when it came to my father, she had less patience for her mother's meddling. I think partly because she did not want my brother and me to hear anything about my father. She looked at my grandmother with pleading eyes, then looked at me, but barely long enough to make eye contact before turning her gaze away.

"If not now, when?"

"Just let the man be."

"I will not let that dog be. I'm always watching him. As long as I have sight, I will never stop watching him. No wonder these boys can't wait to leave."

My father, who was already on his way to the washroom, started walking back towards us. My grandmother stood up, opening herself to the oncoming conflict. My mother's lips were starting to twitch, for fear or anger or pain. I knew she didn't want to have any sort of conversation about my father with my grandmother.

"I want to live with Salomon," said my brother. "I want to finish high school in Strasbourg."

No one was expecting my brother or me to say anything. We were so often relegated to observing them that everyone seemed especially shocked at Junior's request.

"I want to leave Guadeloupe," he said.

My mother looked at him and spoke softly and measuredly. "This is not the time, Junior," she said.

Junior panned from my mother to my father. "You made it clear there's only one king in this house, and I don't want to be at the mercy of no cheating, alcoholic king."

The house went silent. Once and for all, whatever line was drawn in the sand had been crossed. The elephant in the room had ballooned, forcing us all into a corner. My grandmother grabbed on to Junior's hand. My father was less than impressed. His bloodshot eyes unleashed fire towards Junior, his jaw clamped, gnawing at the inside of his mouth. He held his fists tightly in a ball, then turned around without a word and made his way to the shower, slamming the bathroom door.

"You can't worship at church but then not deal with the devil in your house, Widelene," said my grandmother. "This is what happens."

"What happens, Mom? What happens? Just because people talk doesn't make anything true."

Junior stood there, shaking his head.

"Your children are men. They see their father for what he is. There's no place for pride here," said my grandmother.

"On his deathbed, Daddy asked that we not fight, that we keep this family going, that we do what is best for all of us, not just for one," said my mother.

"At what price, Widelene?" asked my grandmother.

"We need to protect the children."

"There are no children here," said my grandmother.

My grandmother's words were curt, but they ultimately, whether my mother believed them or not, rang true. Junior and I may have been my mother's children, but we were no longer needing to be protected and coddled as such. I felt as if four shots were fired that day, or maybe there were five, and I was not sure who the Arab was on the beach.

Chapter 3

Strasbourg, September 1993

Strasbourg. An Alsatian city with a character much like my own. Reserved, timid, its accent unique, all the while drowning itself in much reverie. It was the sort of place that flirted with all inhibition. I likened myself to this inhibition—this new place, new life, new me. Bordering Germany, it was as open to farmland as it was to the Rhine River. I enjoyed my first days there. I thought of Magalie at times and wondered how she found Paris and studying at the Université Paris I. We weren't in touch. Sometimes I wondered if we should have been. Then again, we were not a love story, even if we were more than just friends.

There was a knock on my dormitory door one afternoon as one of my neighbours came to relay that the hallway phone was for me. It was my mother.

"Anyone from home up there?"

"A few. There's a girl on my floor from Saint-François," I said, my tone flat.

"You'll meet more Caribbean folks. You all will find each other," she said, sensing my disinterest in my floormate.

"It irks me when Black people from home act like they don't speak our language," I said. "Every little Black child on any playground speaks Kréyòl. I don't even care if people don't speak it. That's their choice. But don't act like no uppity *chabine* and pretend not to even know it."

"Don't mind those people. They're the same hypocrites who speak French like Spanish cows," she said.

We talked some more about the matter and when I asked about Junior, she said he had been sent home, suspended from school for the day. Apparently, he and his philosophy teacher got into words, and neither the teacher nor the principal particularly liked Junior's words.

"Now I have to go there tomorrow to talk to them, like I have nothing better to do than walk up and down in this heat," she said.

"And Nana?" I asked.

"You know your grandmother. Ticks don't bother cows."

We laughed as she shared some more of my grandmother's antics. I didn't want to ask about my father. I didn't want her to search for words and stumble, like she would in the dark, hit her toe on a wooden bedpost, and cry. But she brought him up.

"You're not going to ask about your father?"

I remained silent.

"Don't let grown people's problems worry you, Salomon," she said after a brief pause.

"I'm not a child, Mom."

"Your father is a good man. He has always provided for you and your brother. No one in this house can say that they have ever gone without because of him."

No one except for her. For the last little while she had been going without. He didn't give her love. He wasn't especially gentle with her. He wasn't respectful of her mother, nor was he kind to her children, especially Junior. His words were hollow and carried no depth. It was hard not to resent him. And if I was beginning to, I knew my brother was well in the throes of lancing grenades and pipe bombs at his head.

Later that evening, early, before the streetlamps came on, I left the student housing complex and made my way down the Wantzenau, a long street flanking one of the many canals which enveloped the city. I was meeting my neighbour Erik and his girlfriend Zara. There was nothing spectacular about the Wantzenau. It served its purpose.

Sometimes there were ducks in the canal, or a stray pig which had drowned and surfed up bloated, decaying on the banks. But that was it. Nothing special or eventful. It was not until I crossed the Rose Blanche Bridge onto Europe Avenue that I felt Strasbourg actually began—where it finally came to life. As I passed the Council of Europe building, the many flags saluted me. A bit further and after one last corner I could see the Palais Universitaire, part of the University of Strasbourg, where we were supposed to meet.

We walked to a brewery close to Cathedral Square. The cathedral itself had been my marker for the past few weeks as I explored the city. If ever I was lost, that's the one monument I knew to look for. I could never adequately describe the cathedral to anyone. It was so much more majestic than any cathedral I had ever seen. To think that men built it to be closer to God, while still pillaging Europe and burning women at the cross, made me wonder about the hearts of men. Their hearts, like the cathedral, were a kind of strange phenomenon.

Similarly, Erik and Zara were not any less strange as a couple. They were two people I would never have put together. My actual first impression of them as a couple was "these two don't go together." Erik was an ethnic Zulu from Durban, South Africa. He had been in Strasbourg for three years, studying interpretation. He arrived on a government scholarship and, in time, would show me the newspaper clipping of his inside-page feature, a picture of him and his parents, proud that he had earned such a prestigious scholarship. His French was perfect. It was flawless. With the exception of his accent and the fact that he rolled his *r*'s at the front of his mouth, he and I spoke the same. He was intelligent, politically astute, and funny. He brought the evening to life, hopelessly attempting to teach Zara and me how to make the clicking sound of his native language at the back of our throats.

As for Zara, she was born and raised in Metz, a town not too far from Strasbourg. Her grandfather Aubain had immigrated to France from French Guiana and married a white French woman. His son, Didier, Zara's father, also married a white woman, and so Zara's complexion was such that if one didn't know her background or wasn't adept at recognising certain cultural characteristics, one could think that she was a white woman. She was awkwardly plain, with long, albeit richly curled black hair that fell down her back. She wore large glasses that, though they suited her face well, seemed rather old. Her style was very simple. Were we living in the 1950s, she would have been considered avant-garde, trying shamelessly to get into the 1980s. Her French was like mine, but more standard of the Continent. There was a hard roll in her *r*'s, as if at any moment she would break out into full German.

Like myself, she was studying in the arts faculty. Interestingly enough, I met Zara before I met Erik, who, by the strangest of all coincidences, ended up being my next-door neighbour on the fourth floor of the student housing complex. As he was a smoker, he found it easier to put his head outside his window to smoke instead of walking down four flights of stairs. If my window was open, the smoke would pervade my small space. One day I stuck my head out in frustration, about to protest the smoke, and was greeted by him telling me about his nicotine addiction. Erik had a captivating air about him, and soon we started hanging out. Most times we would open our windows and chat from the confines of our own rooms as he filled his lungs with tar.

Zara hung on to Erik's every word. He transported her on his own magic carpet. Only the blind would not see the admiration in her eyes. Except for her red lipstick, she wore no makeup. Her face was pale, free of concealer, eye shadow, or blush. Two large hoops dangled from her ears. She was nice enough. Pretty enough, a small mole on her cheek. She laughed and drank with us all the same.

"This is it for me," she said. "I have an early class tomorrow."

It was around ten o'clock, and the time had gotten the better of all of us. As Zara lived close to the square, we proceeded to walk her home, passing by the cathedral.

"We should show Salomon how to really look at the cathedral," she said to Erik.

"I'm not drunk enough for that," he replied.

"Lie down, Salomon." Zara lay on her back, her feet facing the cathedral. "Hurry up! Join me!" she said.

I felt awkward at first, but the alcohol was already flowing through my veins. Erik and I lay on either side of her.

"Now look up!" she said. "Can you see the top?"

I lay there, trying to see the top of the cathedral. Whenever I thought I was seeing it, it was in actuality mere clouds, like gargoyles coming to life and perching on the cathedral roof. I got lost lying there and eventually gave up looking, staring into the night sky, my hands by my side. I felt Zara's hand touch mine, and then her fingers interlock with mine. I reciprocated. Then she let go. When I turned to face her direction, she had mounted Erik and the two were passionately kissing. I had done worse in public places, just not in public. I became uncomfortable as I lay there watching my new friends molest and grope one another, so I got up. But then, that felt uneasy too, and I moved from them. I wanted to say goodbye, but even that seemed awkward. There was nothing I could do that would not make me uncomfortable. So I left. I hopped on the tram all the way back to the Council of Europe building and from there made my way back to the Wantzenau on foot.

The following morning, I didn't see Erik when I left the student housing complex. I assumed he'd spent the night at Zara's. I didn't see her on campus either, not like I always saw her there anyway. But there were many days when our paths crossed, and on those days we took the time to say hello. I was just a bit uncertain of how to act, not sure of my actions from the night before. I was scared that it was I who had grabbed her hand and interlocked our fingers before she pulled her hand away. I was anxious about seeing her.

Upon my return that afternoon, there was a letter addressed to me in my mailbox. Looking at the stamp, I knew it was from Guadeloupe, though it had no return address. The handwriting on the envelope was my brother's. When I got up to my room, I opened it. Strangely, I felt my anxiety bubbling out of me like freshly uncorked champagne out of a bottle on New Year's Eve. I was about to read the letter when someone knocked at my door. I opened it to see Erik and Zara standing there, Erik grinning from ear to ear while Zara just smiled.

"Houdini!" he exclaimed cheekily, mocking my swift disappearance the night before.

We greeted as we customarily did, Erik and I shaking hands, Zara and I kissing each other on the cheek. As she placed her cheek on mine, she rested her hand on my side, just below my rib cage, above my waist, and like a puppy who has been left outside too long and trying to summon its owner to let it back in, she scratched me with her fingers, like a tickle but stronger. They asked that I join them for supper.

We caught the tram to the student cafeteria downtown and afterwards we walked Zara to her residence.

"Who's on duty tonight?" Erik asked her.

"Don't even worry about that," Zara answered, pushing Erik away playfully. "Go home with your friend."

Zara's residence was female only and men were not allowed. However, depending on who the monitor on duty was, the residents snuck in their male counterparts. I watched her as she walked into her building and realised that I watched her too much. She was no longer Zara, Erik's girlfriend, the plain girl from Metz who only wore red lipstick for makeup, her curly black hair so long it touched the small of her back. She had done more than tickle my rib cage. There was something about her I could not articulate back then, but in time I would find the words. I didn't know them that well, and from the outside looking in, they didn't fit. When I looked over at Erik, there was something animalistic about the way he looked at Zara, as if she were this walk-in kitchen pantry with bags of flour and rice, jars of pickles and orange marmalade, copious cans of peaches and coffee. And all he wanted to do was raid that pantry. Part of me felt that he didn't deserve her, or maybe that she deserved better.

Erik and I crossed the square and headed back in the direction of the Palais Universitaire to catch the tram back to the Wantzenau.

"We should go out this weekend," he said. "We won't bring Zara. There's this zouk nightclub. It's called Griot. You'll like it."

Zouk was my staple music in Guadeloupe. So yes, I was sure I would like it.

"There are a lot of women there . . . a lot. Trust me, you won't have to work very hard for it."

"Is that where you met Zara?" I asked.

"Zara doesn't do zouk," he answered, grimacing. "I don't even think she dances at all. I'm actually scared to see her dance."

"So you've never taken her there?"

"Zara is from Metz. There's nothing to do in Metz but look out your window at cows and grains."

I had never been to Metz and was none the wiser.

"She doesn't need to know about Griot," he said. "I've been seeing her for almost a year now. These clubs aren't for her."

We headed towards the tram. I couldn't help but picture my brother in Strasbourg, making new friends in the city, playing football, jumping the tram without paying, being happy. I'd have to find somewhere else to live instead of the dorm. But I knew my mother would never let him leave, not for all the flour or rice or marmalade in the world.

When I got back to the dorm, I sat on my bed and read my brother's letter. It read:

> September 1993, Gwada
>
> Salut Mon Frère,
> I've never had to write a letter in my life, yet here I am writing one to you of all people. It's strange to write to you in French when we only speak Kréyòl between us. It's a shame, isn't it, that we can't write in the tongue we speak. Did you ever have that teacher from Luxembourg, Madame Zeeb, who called Kréyòl "the little negro"? Messed up right? These white people

coming from far away to tell us who we are. I wish you were still here. Gwada's horrible. I don't think I have it in me to follow you and Magalie. I don't have what you have to be able to finish school here. I can't stay quiet and just sit and watch the bullshit happen. Mr. Pelmard can shove his philosophy class up you know where. He thinks he's God's gift to Black people. He talks to us like we don't have a brain in our heads. One of these days, I'll put that man in his place, and I'll have no regrets. Sometimes I wish I was like you and just let stuff roll off my back. I wish I knew how to not let things bother me.

It's getting worse. I feel my skin heat up in anger when these people open their mouths. I can't not react anymore. Every time I try, I feel like I'm being crushed to death. It's just not right. I shouldn't have to be quiet. Even mom is getting on my last nerve. She's not stupid but she's letting dad make a fool out of her. I can't take it man. I want to knock that man in his face and bash his teeth in. I have no respect for him. As far as I'm concerned, I don't have a father anymore. When he's here, he sucks up my space. Mon frère, I know we talked about this before you left, and you said you would look into it, have you? I promise not to be in your way. I can't live here. It was barely tolerable when you were here, but now it's torture. Let me know what you need me to do and I'll do it. Please.

Just me man, Your brother,
Junior

I could hear his voice as I looked down at the words of the letter. If only I had known that letter would be the ghost that would haunt me for the rest of my life.

Chapter 4

Pointe-à-Pitre, December 1993

Feeling the Caribbean sun on my face again reminded me of the time I watched a film with Zara and Erik, and how he and I teased her because "her people" let their dogs lick their faces. She claimed to be equally repulsed by the idea and said that it was not a "Continental French people" issue but rather an American issue and that we should stop watching so much American television. I could only equate the joy of having a slobbering, wet tongue over one's face to the hot sun slobbering over mine.

Truth be told, I had missed my family. I'd missed waking up to my mother and grandmother already in the kitchen grinding their coffee and drinking it with freshly bought baguettes from the bread truck. I even missed the truck, the white wide-back Peugeot, with its feeble horn, like a shy child afraid of speaking up, but just loud enough to make us aware of its presence. I missed everything about the place, even the room I shared with my brother. And yes, I missed him too. It was difficult enough telling him that I couldn't accommodate his request to live with me in Strasbourg.

His appearance had begun to change in those four months since I had last seen him. He now sported a small hoop in his right ear, and on his forearm a tattoo of the name of his dear friend Gaëtan, who died in a motorcycle accident at the end of October. His lips were darker, the white of his eyes a little more red. I knew he smoked Marlboros, but every now and then I'd catch a whiff of marijuana on him. He had hardened. Emboldened. I asked him about it one day.

"Number One son is back," he answered.

My mother instructed him to stop, and then told him he should be more like me.

"Like who?" he asked, putting an unlit cigarette to his mouth. "Why would I want to be so damn square?"

"Boy, respect my house!" she answered. "And take that damn cigarette out of your mouth while you're in my house!"

"Well, you roll the red carpet out for him," he continued.

"Boy, stop talking your crazy nonsense!" said my mother, frustrated with Junior. "You should worry about your education instead of running the streets."

Junior looked impishly at our mother. "Everybody has to run something, Mom."

"Listen to that. He's so smart, he's too smart for his own damn good," she said. "When you run the streets, you don't run anything but to your death."

He ignored my mother. Surprisingly, my grandmother wasn't saying anything. She who threw looks like poisoned spears, she who knew best how to rub salt in an open wound, just sat there, quiet, and only spoke when Junior was just about to exit the front door.

"Don't forget I'm making that crab callaloo for you tonight," said my grandmother. "So don't come home too late to eat. Bring Sandrine. I'm sure your brother would love to meet your girlfriend."

He walked back in, kissed her, and walked out.

"He's clearly not too far gone," my mother said, referring to Junior's tenderness with my grandmother.

"I already told you the boy is angry at the world. You don't listen to me," said my grandmother.

"I don't know how to help him. I don't even know how to talk to him," my mother replied.

I felt her desperation. But this had been brewing for a long time. I hadn't expected it to surface so soon, but there it was. There we were.

"Salomon," my mother said. "I need you to talk to him."

She said this as if I had any power over Junior.

That evening, well after the callaloo had been served, my father walked in. For the few days since I had returned, he'd been getting home consistently late. I was at the table with my mother and grandmother, the latter walking away to the living room as he entered the door. She didn't bother with him. He headed towards the stove. Almost immediately after, Junior walked in as well, looked in my direction and nodded hello, and, as he walked by my mother, passed his hand over her shoulder blades. She turned to look at him as he kept on walking, and I could tell that simple action meant so much to her. He didn't bother to greet my father, who by this time had uncovered the pots of white rice and callaloo.

"I can tell the crabs are Jesula's. She's the only person I know who leaves whole Scotch bonnet peppers in a callaloo," he said.

No one answered. He helped himself and sat at the table with my mother and me. I smelled the rum on his breath. My grandmother walked to Junior's room, and they spoke indiscernibly, after which she came back to the kitchen, fixed him a plate, and brought it to him in the bedroom before returning to her couch.

"Since when does Samuel not eat at this table?" my father asked.

Again, no one answered him.

"Salomon, you see this?" he asked, barely looking in my direction. "Things have changed since you left."

I didn't answer, but in my head I wanted to say, *Yes, they have, you drunk piece of shit!* But I didn't say a word.

"You're not answering either?" he asked as he dug further into his crabs, callaloo all over his beard.

"Come on, Fritzner," said my mother, disgusted. "Do you have to eat it like that? I'm sure Mrs. Destin taught you table manners."

He belched quietly under his breath. He might as well have belched like a drunk at a bar. The stale smell of rum, mixed with callaloo and spicy crab legs, could turn the stomach of any pig.

My mother and I both got up and left, she to my grandmother, me to my brother. Junior was sitting on his bed, his back against the wall, and hadn't touched his plate. It just sat there on the dresser.

"So is Number One going to meet your girlfriend or what?" I asked.

"Nana has to stop telling everybody my business," he answered. "Even Pastor Bishara asked me about her . . . in church."

I laughed.

"We're in line and he's greeting us as we're leaving the church and he's like, 'Did Sandrine not join us today?' He even knew her fucking name," he said.

"And what did you say?"

"Didn't have time to say shit. Nana was all up in there, talking about how the girl lives all the way in Petit-Bourg, so she'll be working on getting her to come out one day."

"Nana has no boundaries, man," I said. "She's always in somebody's business."

"She is too," he acknowledged, shaking his head and laughing. "But that's my girl, though. That's my girl. I love that woman."

That was our grandmother. She would give us hell for taking too long to pee or for opening our mouths too wide to yawn or for the dog's faeces on the sidewalk that lay a little too straight and not crooked enough—for all the things that were not important at all. But she protected us like a lioness protects her cubs. She would raise hell for any one of us.

"She's the only reason I go to church," he said. "And you know how much I hate it."

"Are you sure it's the church or is it Colette Bishara's long mouth you hate?" I asked in jest.

"I don't even look at that woman," he said. "She was bragging about Magalie last Sunday, though. I guess you and her are done."

I knew Magalie had been home a good two weeks before me. I had not seen her since returning and was not really contemplating seeing her.

"We haven't spoken in months. We've *been* done," I replied.

"I know. I wasn't asking. I was just confirming. Mrs. Bishara was bragging because she was so happy that Magalie had brought home a doctor's son—a white boy."

"That would definitely make her happy," I said with a smirk.

"She brought him to church. Most innocent-looking thing south of Paris, I'm sure," he said.

"We'll see how that ends," I said, not feeling hopeful for the French doctor's son.

There was a commotion in the kitchen. My grandmother was screaming at my father, cursing him to hell. Junior and I went to see what the disturbance was about and found my grandmother kneeling over my mother, who had fallen on the floor, imploring her to be strong. Fritzner had left the house.

"That son of a bitch," she said. "What animal comes into your house, eats your food, and tells you he's leaving you? Right before Christmas? What a heartless son of a bitch."

On hearing those words, Junior bolted out the door, my grandmother crying out after him, "Junior! Junior!" Turning to me she yelled, "Go after him! Stop him! Stop your brother!"

She looked at me fiercely, the crescents of smoke in her eyes slowly becoming full moons. They were burning, saying so much more to me than the words she had just spoken.

"That boy got no sense," she muttered with a heavy sigh as she sat on the floor holding my mother in her arms.

That final sigh reinforced everything to me, that I should go after my brother. Her sigh was reflective of her fear that something terrifying was going to happen between Junior and my father. It made me fear it too. As young and fit as Junior was, with a fiery temper that never allowed him to back down for anything or anyone, my father was a big man, and though the years would have slowed him down, Junior would most likely have bitten off far more than he could chew.

I ran outside, and as I approached, I could hear one of the neighbours, Justine, shouting at my father to stop. He was holding Junior by the collar with one hand and with the other ringing the boy's ear with open-handed slaps. Justine was reaching in, trying to get my father to stop, but her effort was as useless as a butterfly swatting at a bear. My father breathed heavily. Junior was furious and was not backing down. And the more he fought to hold his own, the harder the slaps rained on him, falling loud, like giant sheets of plywood on a concrete surface. It was as if my father, perturbed by the insolence of his child, was intent on teaching him a lesson.

I rushed in, putting my body before Junior's, my hands up, ready to stop any further blows. Between Justine and me, we managed to separate them.

My father shouted, "Don't you ever puff your chest at me again, boy. You ever do that again, ever, that will be the last thing you do."

I was restraining Junior, as he was ready to go at my father again. I kept telling him to stop.

"Let him come! Let that jackass come and see what will happen!" said my father, before eventually walking away.

Justine grabbed my brother by the arm and led him under her veranda. She sat him down, clearly repulsed by the swelling on one side of his face. I sat next to him.

"You don't need to be in that house right now. I swear I don't recognise Fritzner anymore. Look at the boy's face," she said, looking at me while shaking her head. "What got into Fritzner? What would make a grown man hit his child like that?"

After a short while, when my brother got up abruptly and said he was heading back home, I went with him, still shaken by what I had just witnessed. As we were nearing the house, my mother and grandmother were making their way out to come find Junior and me. Before my mother could say anything, my grandmother shouted at Junior, her voice trembling more with relief than anger.

"Boy, I already told you, your temper will kill you. When stray dogs go piss in the woods, you let them. You don't go after them. Look at your face!" she said. The horror in her eyes echoed in my mother's.

Junior didn't answer. My mother could barely look at him as he walked past them. When he entered his bedroom, he slammed the door, and we heard a plate crash against the bedroom wall. My grandmother looked at us, flustered, clearly wanting to do something. Instead, she closed her eyes and put her hands on her chest, looked towards the sky.

"Jesus, help my child. Heal him, Lord," she said. She looked back at my mother.

"That poor boy. All I can do for him is pray. This isn't right, Widelene. Prayer shouldn't be the best that we can do."

My father didn't come home that night. Good thing too, for I don't know where he would have slept. I couldn't imagine he would have slept next to the person whom he, just a few hours earlier, had told he was leaving. And I slept on the couch in the living room, not wanting to bother Junior, nor did I want to sleep with the smell of callaloo in my nostrils all night. Surely, my father would not sleep in the bedroom with Junior. And as for my grandmother, forget it. Maybe outside under the veranda, like the stray dog that he was.

I was still sleeping the next morning when my grandmother, carrying a bucket full of Clorox, started cleaning the callaloo off the walls in the bedroom. I awoke to her and my mother talking loudly, as if they were out at the butcher's asking about the price of a porterhouse steak, as if I wasn't lying there sleeping.

I didn't see my father the entire day. Word had gotten out about him and Junior, but no one knew the reason why—just us. A few neighbours came down to see if we were all right. Some were genuinely concerned, others just looking for gossip. I was seated in the living room when I heard a light knock on the door, and my mother inviting the person in. It was Magalie.

"This is Léo," I heard Magalie say.

I could tell by my mother's voice that she wasn't pleased with Magalie bringing Léo to the house, but she did not want to be rude. My grandmother, who had been gently swaying back and forth in the rocking chair across from me, stopped rocking and listened, shaking her head.

"You've seen her yet, since you got back?" my grandmother asked me softly.

I shook my head.

"These people have no shame," she said, again softly.

"I saw you two at church last Sunday. Is this your first visit to Guadeloupe, Léo?" my mother asked.

"She better not ask them to sit down," my grandmother whispered.

"No. I haven't been here in a few years. We vacation on Saint Bart's often," Léo replied.

"Oh God!" whispered my grandmother. "He's one of those." She got up and headed to the kitchen.

"Well, I just came to see if Junior was OK."

"He's fine. Thank you for checking in on him. You know, families go through their things. In time I'm sure he and his father will work it out," said my mother.

"Hello, Magalie," said my grandmother. Magalie didn't have a chance to reply before she continued speaking. "You know the rain is coming tonight? You don't want to be caught in it." My grandmother was clear in her feelings towards Magalie, her words forceful.

"Well, tell Junior and Salomon I said hi. They're not home, are they?" she asked.

"No, they're not," answered my grandmother.

Junior wasn't home, but I was there, sitting in the other room. I liked how my grandmother took care of business. Frankly, I wasn't sure my mother was up to the task.

"Well, maybe I'll see them at church tomorrow?"

"Maybe," my grandmother answered.

Magalie and Léo left. I wanted to see for myself what her boyfriend looked like more than I wanted to see her. Christmas was in a week, and I was bound to see her sooner or later. I figured I might as well go to church in the morning.

By the time I went to bed, my father had still not come home.

Chapter 5

When we entered the church the next morning, we sat several rows behind Magalie—my grandmother, my mother, Junior, and me. My mother looked radiant. The pattern of her yellow dress hugged her brown skin. Before leaving the house, we'd told her she looked so good that she should consider staying in her dress all day.

Magalie sat in her usual front-row pew with her mother and brother and was accompanied this time by Léo. I could only see the back of his head. He didn't move much and was rather stoic in his seat, unlike Magalie, who kept looking back at the other side of the church, where my family usually sat. I wanted to think she was looking for me, but not because I cared. It just made me feel somewhat powerful, like I had an edge over Léo. I could tell that he was shorter than I was, and thinner. I wondered if he was uncomfortable. I didn't imagine he was used to cramped evangelical churches on Sundays, in a sweltering heat, or being the lone white man in a sea of Black sweat, with preservice chatter in French and Kréyòl. I wondered if deep down he even wanted to be there, at church, and maybe with Magalie. She kept looking backwards, and finally looking directly behind her, she caught my gaze. She half smiled and gave a wave so small, it was hardly noticeable.

"Who taught her to wave, the queen of England?" my grandmother asked, unimpressed.

"She just better focus on Jesus," said my mother.

My grandmother and Junior laughed under their breath. I didn't laugh but instead forced out a smile.

During the service, all I could think about was how not to make the after-service greeting uncomfortable—for me. I was thinking of something I could say that would make Magalie uneasy, something about our history, that only she and I would know, something that would go over Léo's head. But I was equally worried that it would backfire, as she was full of wit and quick of tongue. I didn't hear anything that Pastor Bishara said. When it was over, I was just as happy to have survived it. I didn't miss these services. I would have one more at Christmas and then I'd be gone back to Strasbourg before the New Year.

"This is my friend Salomon and his brother Junior," she said to Léo as she introduced us to each other.

I saw his face for the first time. There was nothing particular about him. I doubted if he played any sort of aggressive sport, or if he had ever strained in his life. He wasn't muscular, just full of bones, as far as I could see. I was thoroughly satisfied and at the same time quite unimpressed.

"Have you taken him to the school yet?" I asked.

Magalie immediately caught on to what I was doing and replied just as I feared she would. "The school doesn't compare to Paris," she said. "So there's no point."

When we got home, my father was waiting under the veranda. He had obviously been in the house, having showered and cleaned up while we were at church. He ignored everyone except for my mother.

"Widelene," he said, grabbing her arm. She pulled away, but he insisted. "Widelene."

"Widelene what?" she asked. "You can't even say hello to your children? They're right there. Right there! So don't bloody Widelene me nothing!"

"I need to talk to you." He was pleading.

"You talked plenty already two days ago. And then you, a grown man, was rolling around on concrete in front of Sonya and Gervais's front step with your fifteen-year-old son, slapping the boy like you slapping some dog. What could you possibly have to say?"

When she made her way into the house, he tried following her. "Don't you set foot in my house!" she shouted. "Don't you dare!"

Sulking, my father remained under the veranda as my mother stormed into the house and went into her bedroom. A short while later, she came into the kitchen, having changed out of the Sunday dress. Junior also had changed and left the house, not saying a word to anybody. No one asked either. We were three in the kitchen, my father on the threshold of our doorstep, the same one he had built with his very own hands. He stood there, his tail between his legs, like a famished dog waiting for scraps.

"Widelene! Come on, man," he said.

She turned to face him, dish towel in her hand and hands, turned in at the wrists, on her hips. My father stood in the doorway, his own hands grabbing the doorframe, one foot in, the other out.

"I told you already not to call my name," she replied.

"I was drunk," he said.

"You're always drunk. You've been drunk for a long time."

My grandmother and I were quiet, looking on.

"So you're really not going to talk to me?" he asked.

"I already told you I have nothing to say to you. You should grab what you need and go back to wherever the hell you came from. I don't care."

My father eventually left, but my mother was still angry. "Oh holy God," she said. "In the name of Jesus, please give me strength to put this man out of my mind and off of my tongue."

And then, as her frustration settled and her shaking stopped, she was able to breathe again. The three of us talked about Christmas and how we should have it on the beach. How we could organise with the neighbours and spend the day there after the church service. My grandmother reminisced about how when she and my grandfather first came to Guadeloupe, they, along with other Haitian friends, would even cook at the beach on Christmas, spit roasting an entire goat and having the time of their lives. My mother remembered those days as a child and that it was on one such occasion that she fell in love with the Guadeloupe bread pudding. She regretted never doing that with us.

We didn't see my father again until the Thursday before Christmas Eve. The neighbours all knew there was a rift between my parents. They also knew the reason for this rift, just as they knew where my father was staying and with whom. They've always known, the same way my grandmother has always known, like I have, like Junior. Even my mother knew, though she pretended not to. But now, there was no pretending. It slapped her in the face every time she stepped outside the house.

My father entered the house, not caring what anybody had to say, made his way to my mother's bedroom, and shortly after, came out rather perturbed.

"Where's all my stuff?" he asked.

"Why don't you ask Wednesday? Maybe Tuesday and Monday will tell you," my mother answered.

"I don't know what nonsense you're talking. That's all the clothes I own, Widelene."

"They're in the cardboard box by the table, outside under the veranda. It's probably wet from Monday's rain. Watch out for the roaches," she said.

He tried to get the box, but it fell apart. I could hear him cursing under his breath.

From the distance I could see Junior approaching, holding hands with a girl whom I could only imagine to be Sandrine. No one else noticed Junior. I was not sure what his reaction would be upon seeing our father, but if I knew one thing it was that Fritzner Destin was the last person Junior wanted to see. In the meantime, my mother must have been feeling some way for my father. Maybe she felt sorry for him or was just eager for him to leave. She fetched some plastic grocery bags for him to use instead of him carrying the wet cardboard box.

I ventured outside and walked towards Junior and Sandrine. I wasn't sure what I was going to say, but in my bones I knew I had to warn him somehow. We greeted and he introduced me to Sandrine. I could see why my grandmother was so boastful about her. She evoked a particular sweetness, her face beautifully dimpled like the surface of the moon, her brown skin just bars of gold glowing under a dim light, the scent of cocoa butter emanating from her pores.

"He's getting his stuff," I said to Junior. "Under the veranda."

I could tell Junior was annoyed. He acknowledged the information and continued to the house with Sandrine. By the time we got there, my father had entered the house and was arguing with my mother. My grandmother was trying to get him to leave.

"This is my house, Jesula, my house," he kept repeating. "I built this house with my own two hands. I'll be damned if I let you tell me if I am or am not allowed in it."

My father had not been drinking, so his words to my grandmother were like barbed wire tearing at my skin.

"So you can go to hell, you old blood-sucking soukounian!" he said to her.

I felt embarrassed for Junior, who was at the door with Sandrine. I would have rather he be embarrassed of me, the Number One, the inglorious square.

And then the most dumbfounding of events happened. Junior rushed in and cracked my father on the jaw with his fist. Chaos. But in that moment, I heard nothing but silence. Amid the commotion, my brain was embroiled in a fog of disbelief.

"Stop him, Salomon!" my mother shouted.

I regained clarity and saw my father lying on the ground, shielding himself as best he could from Junior, who was kicking him repeatedly, with all the rage in his body. I grabbed Junior from the back and pulled him away from our father. Sandrine was standing at the door, visibly shaken, her eyes darting from Junior to my father, to my mother and my grandmother, to me, and back to Junior, seemingly unable to comprehend what had just happened. My grandmother was calm, but my mother was screaming, asking when had the devil entered the house. She wanted to know when we had become so dysfunctional.

"Where there's smoke, there's fire, girl," my grandmother said to my mother, her voice stern. "Where there's sin, there's the devil."

Then she looked at my father, still lying on the ground holding his face. "That boy is going to pay for your sins, Fritzner. The devil is out for his pound of flesh."

My father was taken to the hospital, where his jaw was wired shut. He was released on Christmas Day, the ambulatory services bringing him home to us, the address he had on file, giving his medication and care instructions to his next of kin, my mother.

"You know she brought me your clothes," my mother said to him after she sat him down on the couch. "She brought me everything . . . your work boots, your razor, even your toothbrush."

My father sat there, at the mercy of my mother, my grandmother across from him in her rocking chair. Her eyes were closed, and she did not open them once to look at him. She just kept on rocking.

"Your mistress doesn't want you," my mother continued telling my father. "She doesn't want to take care of you. Junior refuses to live under the same roof as you. Your son . . . my child is gone because of you. I have to take care of you. Me. *I* have to take care of you. But you hear me well—when you heal, I do not want you living here. I even missed my Christmas service for you. If God wasn't good, I don't know where you would be right now."

Christmas was not spent at the beach as we had discussed. There was no bread pudding, no goat on an open pit. Our family was in turmoil, and I didn't know how I would leave my mother and grandmother in the state they were in. I was leaving in a few days, and I felt uneasy about it. At least Junior was safe. He went to live with a close friend of the family in Baie-Mahault, closer to Sandrine. We had asked my father's sister who lived near us to take him in for a few months, but she refused.

"I don't have to go back, Mom," I said to my mother. "I can stay until this situation is figured out and Junior comes back home."

"No," she replied. "You will do no such thing."

"Mom, how am I supposed to leave with how things are here? I feel like I need to help."

"Help do what? What exactly do you plan on helping?"

"Anything."

My mother rested a hand on my knee and looked into my eyes. "Go back to Strasbourg. That's the only thing you can do right now."

I wanted to believe her, but I could also feel my grandmother judging me and expecting me to stay. Even if it meant feeding my father soup through a straw, I felt I could be doing something. A knock at the door interrupted my conversation with my mother.

"Merry Christmas!" my mother said, opening the door for Magalie and inviting her in.

After we all greeted, Magalie said, "This is for you, Mrs. Destin," and handed my mother a bread pudding encased in Tupperware. "I know how much you like it."

"I do! Thank you so much," my mother replied.

"I asked my Aunt Marie-Pierre to make it with the extra-soft rum raisins," said Magalie.

She, my mother, and grandmother talked briefly about the Christmas service and Magalie's family. I don't think my mother and grandmother were particularly interested in her family, just that they were appreciative of Magalie's kindness and were being courteous in return.

"Well, join us for some tea," said my grandmother. "Your auntie makes the best bread pudding. Can't wait to have some."

She graciously declined, citing that she had to rescue Léo from her mother. I was surprised he wasn't with her and was wondering how come neither my mother nor grandmother enquired about him. My mother then instructed me to walk Magalie home. Magalie tried to refuse, but there was no point.

"Child, I would never forgive myself if anything happened to you tonight when you leave here," my mother said.

So it was settled, and Magalie and I left. It was a ten-minute walk if pressed, though all the times she and I had walked it, it had taken us much longer than that. That evening would be no different.

"How's your dad coping having to eat soup for the next month?" she asked as we walked.

"He can't really complain," I answered. "And he's trying to be perfect for my mom."

"You think she'll take him back?"

"She has," I said. "I mean, he's in the house already. He's not going anywhere."

Until tonight I hadn't thought about that, so I surprised myself to have articulated it so readily.

"It's ironic, the straw that broke the camel's back. And there he is with a bag of straws that she needs to feed him with," she said.

"You sound like my grandmother. She said if it were up to her, she would never change straws and have him suck out of the same old nasty straw every day. And really he would never know any better."

"Jesula has that old-school Haitian take-no-prisoner mentality. She don't play. She's the type to bring out an axe when you slap her. She doesn't give a shit," said Magalie.

She was right. My grandmother could have been a hit man for a mob or a mob boss herself. She always said that she was too old to give a damn what people thought about her.

"She basically told me to fuck off last time I came down," she said.

"I heard her," I said.

"So you *were* there?"

"Yes," I said, grinning.

"I fucking knew it. She can be such a . . ." she said, not completing her thought.

"I know. You should live with her. Is that why you didn't bring Léo tonight?"

Magalie took a deep breath before answering me. "He's not stupid, you know. He asked about the school. And I was so humiliated last time, he kind of put two and two together."

"I'm sorry," I said. "I didn't really care, but at the same time I was jealous. I can't explain it."

"I guess I could have given you a heads-up."

I didn't think it would have mattered what she had done. Some feelings just never truly go away. My feelings for her were some of those very ones.

"Is Junior going to be OK?" she asked.

"He will be. He is closer to school and to his girlfriend. One of them will make him happy, though I doubt it will be school," I answered.

"Your poor mom."

"You mean, my poor *Christian* mom?" She looked at me not understanding, and I explained. "The love she has for Christ asks that she love my father and that she forgive him."

"And Junior?" she asked.

"That same love asks that she sacrifice and compromise for the greater good," I answered.

Magalie sighed. "Poor Junior."

"I wouldn't feel so bad about it all if I felt he didn't understand the implications of my mother's actions."

"Ugh!" She sighed again.

"Yeah. Exactly. He's no dummy. He's thought this out a million times in his head. He understands it all too well."

We were walking on the final stretch of road before turning onto her street. There was a melancholy between us, marred further by the darkness of the night. The streetlamps worked few and far between. "I can't believe Widelene is fine with me walking back home alone in this frigging darkness," I said.

Magalie stopped in front of me, her face close enough to mine I could have kissed her without moving my head. "You know I couldn't give a shit about who likes bread pudding, right?"

I felt the heat of her breath as her lips grazed mine. I could not see the colour of her eyes in the darkness, but I felt ensorcelled nonetheless. I kissed her. She didn't move away, but she didn't kiss me back. I paused, pulled back.

She said, "My body is on fire right now. So if you're only going to kiss me, then just walk me the rest of the way home and let me be."

I kissed her again. And when she reciprocated, the hair stood on my arms. I could feel my veins harden, blood pumping through them like pistons pumping diesel through a turbo engine. As we kissed further and more intensely, we found ourselves waltzing quasi-violently off the street. And there we were, a displaced figure in the darkness between two houses. We did not belong. We were thieves, stealing each other's breaths, molesting our shades of brown skin, reclaiming our time—reclaiming us. We could hear the television sets blasting from inside. People were talking, children laughing, screaming. I realised I had not cared how loud I was, that is until she cupped my mouth with one hand, holding on to me with the other, all the while controlling her own moaning. All I could think about was her bare skin, my hand through her blouse, under her skirt, the lining of her panties. I had craved this moment for such a long time. I had wanted her. I finally had my moment, but time would tell if I would have her.

The following day, I visited my brother in Baie-Mahault. He was alone when I got to the house, opting not to join the family on their Boxing Day excursion. Our greeting was wanting, our words sparse. I felt a strangeness in him. I pitied him. If I was Number One, he was the Exiled One, forced to live on the fringes of all of us.

"How's Nana?" he asked.

"She's fine," I answered.

Truth is, she and my mother were complicated. They did not see eye to eye on this situation. According to my grandmother, children should not be made to carry the sins of their father. But my mother saw it differently. To her, whatever was happening between her and my father was between them, and Junior had no right to break the man's jaw. But it made no point getting into that.

"When do you leave again?" he asked.

"Tomorrow night," I answered. I was landing in Paris and taking the TGV, the country's high-speed train, into Strasbourg.

"So, you get to escape the nightmare."

"It's not like life pauses for me. I'll still be over there worrying about all of you."

"Uh-huh," he said, offering that we sit at the table outside under the veranda.

He lit a cigarette.

"You know I'm not going back there, right?" he asked, seeking confirmation.

I feared he would feel that way.

"Fuck that place!" he said. "After all that motherfucker's done, she just lets him back in. And *I* have to leave? You'll never see me there again."

"It's complicated, though," I tried reasoning.

He was not hearing any of it. To him, there was no complication. To him, fathers were assholes, and their behaviour was to be expected. But mothers were supposed to protect their children, not choose miserable and hapless old dogs over them.

"You can't stay here forever," I said.

"Don't worry about me. They won't have to worry about me either."

In the hours that ensued sitting under the veranda, it was clear to me that Junior's mind was made up. The hardest part was talking to him without preaching, he having already reproached me for doing so.

"You're my brother," he said. "Act like it. I don't need another father."

I had no solution to offer, except to just listen to him, a task I found particularly difficult since most of the time I found myself wondering how I was going to manage being all right a world and an ocean away, when he was anything but all right. He had already changed so much in the first few months of me leaving, I could only imagine how much he will have changed by my return in June.

As for my father, there was an unspoken rule that one should never insult his wife's mother, no matter how miserable she made him. He was to complain to his wife and then shut up about it. But calling my grandmother a soukounian—the most grotesque and vile of island sorcery—was beyond any fathomable measure of redemption.

Chapter 6

Strasbourg, December 1993

I left the Strasbourg train station around noon, exhausted, jet-lagged, and cold. I contemplated taking a taxi to my residence, but I was hungry and knew with absolute certainty that there was nothing to eat in my room. I hopped on the tram into the city centre, figuring I would find food there and bring something to the residence that I could have after I awoke from my death.

I didn't get home until around three in the afternoon. I don't remember undressing or even hitting my bed, just waking up the next day with someone knocking at my door.

"*Téléphone!*" the voice said through the door.

I knew it was my mother. I also knew she was upset that I hadn't called her the day before to let her know I had arrived safely. I was so tired, I had forgotten. And sure enough, it was my mother. Sure enough, she was upset. But I suppose that's what mothers do. They worry when they don't even need to.

There was no one around to hang out with. Zara and Erik were both out of town. Zara had gone to visit her family in Metz and was due to return soon, perhaps already having done so. Erik and a few of the other African boys had gone south to Montpellier to visit their friend for Christmas. They were to return for the New Year, as was the plan, for us all to party. Erik couldn't go home to Durban. It was too far and did not make any economic sense. He wasn't alone. The other guys with him were in the same situation, whether it was Mali, Togo, or the Congo. They stayed in France and made the best of the situation. Some did not celebrate Christmas anyway, so going home was never an issue.

Erik called and let me know that he and the others would not be returning to Strasbourg before the New Year. He invited me down to Montpellier, stressing there was plenty of room. I told him I would consider it, even though deep down I knew my mind was already made up and that I wouldn't be going to Montpellier. Further, I knew, depending on our circumstances, "plenty of room" could be quite relative. No doubt they would have a fun time, and I imagined them being up to no good. Montpellier would not know what hit it that New Year's Eve, not until those boys were on the TGV back to Strasbourg. Erik did, however, provide me with the phone number to Zara's residence, in case I wanted to touch base with her. He said that if I chose not to come down to meet them, then Zara and her friends would most certainly be doing something to celebrate the New Year and that I should join them. I wasn't keen on the idea of joining her friends, but I was keen to see and hang out with her.

We met at Kleber Square the following afternoon. She wanted to treat herself to a few books from a bookstore there. Upon seeing her, I looked her up and down again, and, as before, there was nothing overly special about her figure or appearance. But she was kind and laughed easily and, like me, found the most mundane of things interesting. I would be disingenuous if I said I didn't carry a torch for her. I was a bit nervous, even awkward upon seeing her again. I'm sure my nerves betrayed my composure. She remained unmoved as we entered the store and made small talk. Curious about Metz, I asked her about adapting to life in Strasbourg. She looked at me, a bit perplexed.

"I thought being from a farming community, living in a city would need some adjustment," I said, qualifying my question.

"Because I look like a farmer's daughter?" she asked, grimacing.

"No . . . well . . . Erik . . ."

"Erik? Erik has never been to Metz. For whatever reason, he associates it with cows and farmland. Metz is not that different from Strasbourg, just about a third smaller in size." She seemed annoyed, not at me but at Erik's misrepresentation of her hometown.

"I most likely misunderstood him," I said. "We were at the brewery at the time."

She didn't respond, just continued perusing, showing me her favourite section as well as the music catalogue.

"Erik never comes in here with me," she said. "He never reads for pleasure. So many great books out there, I could never imagine not reading for pleasure."

I didn't read for pleasure either, but somehow, she assumed that I did as she confirmed the ridiculousness of those who didn't take time to read.

"Reading is such a privilege. Imagine if we couldn't read about our history. Imagine all the things we would never know about this city, even. What if we had no idea about the Oaths of Strasbourg," she said.

I had never heard of this oath, and so she explained it to me, of the two brothers, Louis and Charles, kings of East and West Francia respectively, who, after defeating their brother Emperor Lothair in 841, swore allegiance to each other a year later in front of their respective armies, in the other's tongue, binding them together against him. She didn't care much for the details, just that it preceded the Treaty of Verdun, and as she was scholarly, she remarked that the oaths were the first sign of East and West Francia not sharing a common language.

"It was the start," she said, "of Europe dividing, of France and Germany." It was the start, all right, I thought, losing myself in her.

We spent about an hour in the bookstore before we made our way across the square to a Häagen-Dazs café. As we passed a few clothing stores along the way, she shook her head in distaste.

"Does it bother you that the security guards are all Black?" she asked.

"They have to eat. I can't blame them for finding ways to put food in their mouths," I replied.

"You know what I mean," she said. "Look all around the square. Doesn't that just grate your insides?"

It's not that it didn't bother me. I suppose I was not affected as viscerally as she was. I could understand her displeasure, looking at our people represented in that way. They were guards standing at the front of the stores, various shades of the same dark complexion, loaded like cocked firearms, intending to project fear as much as they proposed safety and security. They were no different than German shepherds on a leash. I felt her rage affecting me—a quiet rage, but a rage nonetheless, like a brewing subversion, the need to cause a scene and disrupt the way things were.

"I want to pull these men from the storefronts. I want to pull them like I was pulling their Black bodies from a fire," she said.

That image struck me, for they were burning. I wondered if they felt the heat. Their Blackness was being used as a weapon against them. It was in fact a weapon against our collective Blackness, one which was portrayed as ugly, weak, and damagingly subservient. But there it was, standing guard, intently menacing. I had long understood the sugarcane fields of Guadeloupe. I had long understood the sweaty Black bodies working in them under the scorching sun, the white owner of the fields—the *béké*—cashing in on the sugar and the rum they produced. I understood all that. I used to see it every day. That is, after all, one of the reasons I had resigned myself never to work in any field cutting any *béké's* cane. I was well aware of the white man's power in Guadeloupe, well aware of the colonial structures. But for Zara, it looked different. Here in Strasbourg, our Black bodies were again stolen from us, painted in a hue of intimidation and villainy, so well masked that many of us did not even see it. We had become vicious watchdogs at the entrance of the white man's stores.

We sat down at the Häagen-Dazs café. She turned her nose up at my rum raisin scoop.

"You and Erik are so different," she said.

"He doesn't like rum raisin ice cream either?" I asked.

"I mean, in matters of race and identity," she said. "You said that they had to eat. Erik would look down on them as pathetic. To him, you need to have dignity—even if you're poor, you should still be dignified."

I didn't dispute that, and I knew that she didn't either.

"I guess you're more empathetic than he is," she said.

We ate, all the while looking at each other playfully, quasi-flirtatiously.

"Say what's on your mind," she advised, acknowledging that I had something rumbling in the back of my head.

"If two people are different, it's you and Erik," I said.

"We are," she said with laughter.

After a few minutes, we decided to leave. As we walked out into the cold air, she grabbed my arm and pulled herself into me. We crossed the square in the direction of the bookstore where we had just been. I could smell the scent of her hair. It was that of a fragrance that arose from the bosom of the earth, destined for the breaths of those like me, men and women who were enticed by the colours of smell. She was feminine in ways I had not considered, her plainness a distraction to the eroticism she yielded.

Two days later, we met by the steps of the Palais Universitaire. She had invited me as her guest to a party hosted by one of her friends to ring in the New Year. When she said "party," in my mind I envisioned a "soirée" and not my typical New Year's Eve celebration. I knew that the boys in Montpellier were not at any kind of soirée, and I envied them. New Year's Eve in Montpellier was going to be wild. I was curious if Zara ever wondered about Erik, the ease with which he pulled people to him, the way women admired him and were drawn to him.

"I didn't imagine Strasbourg to be so quiet on New Year's Eve," I said to her.

"It's not that quiet," she answered. "People will be out and about. But no, it's not Paris. If you want fireworks, you'll have to cross the Rhine into Germany."

"In Kehl? That little town?" I scoffed, unable to imagine it.

She laughed, acknowledging my surprise. "The Christmas market is really nice. Had we been here around Christmas, I would have taken you."

When we entered, the host, Brielle, looked us up and down and smirked. "This is interesting. I like this combination. But don't mind me, I have a bad record of good coupling," she said.

Zara introduced us, and then introduced me to the rest of the guests, who for the most part were sitting down, having wine and what seemed as the most boring time of their lives. I was reluctantly greeting people at a party I didn't really want to be attending. I realised I may have made a mistake in not meeting Erik and the others in Montpellier. I had an urge to celebrate and be joyous, not to be stuck in an apartment, listening to stories about people's Alsatian grandmothers and their accents, about where to find the best tarte flambée, the Alsatian quiche, and whatever other stories that did nothing to illuminate my night.

As the evening progressed, Zara and I fell into conversation with her friend Anouk and Anouk's boyfriend, Maxim. Anouk was our age, Black, her figure much fuller than Zara's. She was born in France, though her family had immigrated from Côte d'Ivoire. Her boyfriend, Maxim, was white and considerably older. Zara was particularly cold to him, which made me immediately apprehensive of him.

"We're not staying much longer," he said. "We're meeting some of my friends in a bit. This crowd is a bit young."

"Well, when an almost thirty-year-old is dating a twenty-year-old, it's not that the twenty-year-old's crowd is young, it's that the almost thirty-year-old is almost thirty years old," Zara answered.

He ignored her and went to use the washroom.

"Zara, we had a deal," said Anouk. "If I can't talk about Erik, you can't talk about Maxim."

"I wasn't talking about him. I was talking to him."

"Semantics."

"Almost thirty-year-old semantics."

"Shut up."

They laughed, but clearly neither, for whatever reason, liked the other's boyfriend. When Anouk and Maxim left, Zara and I felt that we should too.

"I thought this would have been more fun," she said to me. "I don't do nightclubs, but I'd do one right now."

She said this in jest, but the idea appealed to me.

"Are they even open?" I asked.

"It's Friday night on New Year's Eve. I imagine they're open," she answered.

We smiled at the prospect of doing something a bit more exciting that night. At this point I didn't care if it was hanging out in the cold at Kleber or Cathedral Square. Anything had to be more exciting than this. I proposed that we leave.

"That would be rude," she said, the expression on her face showing her regret. She sensed my dread. "What would we say?"

"Nothing. Fuck it. These people and their bullshit party."

She laughed, then sensing I was serious, laughed some more. She put the palm of her hand on my cheek and brought it down over my chest. She grinned, excited. We left in silence, laughing our way down the flights of stairs. We exited the building and ran hand in hand as if someone was going to chase us and drag us back up there. When we stopped, I pulled her into me. We both breathed a heavy sigh, our faces inches away from each other's.

"You're Erik's friend," she said.

I was enthralled by the smell of her hair and her perfume, her sweet breath, infused modestly with wine. "We all have friends," I said.

I didn't even know what that meant or even if it made sense. I don't imagine she did either. But it was better than what I wanted to say, that Erik would never know.

"Some lines I wish I could cross," she said.

I wanted to devour her.

"Well, the night's young. There's still time for that," I blurted.

We both laughed and made our way to the centre of town.

Downtown Strasbourg was well lit. People were everywhere. It was certainly not as quiet as I had thought. Zara and I were arm in arm the entire way, at times even holding hands. I didn't care for her lines, those imaginary boundaries that she would not cross. It was she who flirted and touched me covertly. She wanted more. I wanted more. I didn't believe she was in love with Erik. Or maybe she was. Maybe I was *that* friend, the one you couldn't trust.

We arrived at an intersection leading to a bar on each street. I invited her to pick a street, and whatever she picked, we would go to the bar there. "If you don't like it, we won't stay," I said.

"I'll keep an open mind. I'll try it. The night is young, right?" she teased.

She chose a street, but I overruled her. "Your first should not be by chance. It should be with someone who knows what they're doing," I said.

She shook her head, smiling. "Experience is so overrated."

We entered Griot. It wasn't overly packed, but crowded nonetheless. I could tell she liked the ambiance.

"Is this where you and Erik hang out?" she asked.

I nodded. I recognised that I was betraying Erik. He would have never brought her there. Zara and I stood by the bar and had a drink. I explained zouk music to her and how you could tell the difference between zouk from Martinique and Guadeloupe and zouk from Haiti, how to tell if music was African or not. She listened and after a few songs could distinguish some differences. She was looking at the dance floor as the dancers held their partners intimately. She asked if people always danced to zouk with a partner.

"Yes. Always . . . well, most times. Drunk men tend to dance alone. They don't even need music."

Then I took her hand and pulled her onto the dance floor. It was a slow song. "This is my favourite kind of zouk. We call it Zouk-love."

She didn't have time to refuse. She put her arms around my neck in a tight embrace, my hands on both the upper and lower part of her back, one leg between her thighs and hers between mine.

"The man always leads," I said.

She let me lead. It was a song I had danced to countless times, with dancers more fluid than she was. Her feet were not smooth, but in my hands she felt like satin sheets, pressed against me by the wind. I held her tighter and she tightened her grip. The song finished and neither of us moved. Another started and we danced again. Zouk was sensual. It was public foreplay, lingerie for the purpose of sexual gratification.

It was nearing midnight—the night still young—when we left the bar. We walked to Cathedral Square, but I could hardly feel the cold. As we got close to where we had lain in front of the cathedral, that night with Erik, I told her how awkward and uncomfortable it was, me looking at her and Erik make out.

"Jealousy can be uncomfortable," she said, smiling.

I didn't answer.

"So it's true?" she affirmed. "You were jealous."

"No. It's not true. I just wonder what line will be crossed when I kiss you at midnight."

We were acting like lovers, hand in hand, arm in arm, talking, smiling, caressing, hugging. Anyone who saw us would think we were a couple, but we weren't, and I was tired of the game. One of us was prey, could have been either one, but now, clearly, the pursuit was done, and in that moment I didn't care about Erik or any imaginary line drawn in the sand.

"You don't have to wait until midnight," she said.

Within mere minutes to midnight, I kissed her. She hung on to my lips, her tongue feeling the inside of my mouth, reaching deeper and deeper as if searching for a soft place to rest. Then there was clapping all around us. The cathedral clock had struck twelve and the crowd acknowledged the New Year. They could have been clapping for us.

"There's no concierge on duty tonight," she said, referring to her residence. "But you'll have to leave by eight."

I didn't care if I had to leave by three in the morning and had to walk the Wantzenau in the darkness. I was hungry for her. I wanted to see her naked body. I had imagined it under her clothes, and I could see under the plainness that she held a glorious womanhood, her femininity one of fullness and curves.

Her room was empty like mine, with only the necessities of student life. From her second-floor window, we watched people in the streets heading to and from the square. I had expected things to move along faster once in her room, but now that we were there, time lulled like uncomfortable small talk. She was hesitant, wanting to say something. I knew it was about Erik, and I didn't want to bring him up, not right then. And then I surprised myself with my own words.

"I shouldn't have kissed you. I shouldn't have tempted you to be unfaithful to your boyfriend."

We stood by the window, and I could tell she was uncertain of what to do, but also that she wanted me to stay. I reached out my hand and asked her if I should leave. She shook her head, approached me, and we kissed again.

I had never had the liberty of being with a woman knowing that I didn't have to rush, or that at any time someone would walk in, not having to listen for voices or footsteps. For the first time I was safe from being found out, or caught, or chased away. And for the first time, Zara revealed her body to me. Her pale skin felt rich in the dimly lit room, like the translucent shavings of dark wood, with blemishes and scars, pockmarks and moles, a birthmark near her navel. They were all accents of a well-curated skin, her full lips against her light eyes, like the fusion of the *choucroute alsacienne* and the *boucanage guyanais*. The moon over Strasbourg did more than illuminate the night sky. It pulled tightly on her curves, so much fuller than I had dared to imagine.

The following morning, we lay on her bed, both of us still naked from the night before.

"Would you ever be with a white woman?" she asked.

"I have no objections to white women," I answered. "Why?"

"When you see me, do you see a white woman?"

"Of course not."

In our past conversations about race, she had explained to me how her father and grandfather had instilled in her the importance of having pride in her Blackness.

"Would you go out with a white guy?"

"I don't know. I don't think so. I mean, remember I told you about my dad and grandpa, and how they're so proud of being Black?"

"Yeah."

"Yet they both married white women. Why marry a white woman if you're so proud to be Black?" she asked.

"I don't think the two are mutually exclusive," I said. "You just have to pick the right person."

I realised it was difficult for her, so obviously belonging to two cultures.

"It bothers me to think that I would knowingly contribute to white supremacy by not being with a Black man," she said.

I didn't respond. I took it in silently.

"Too much too soon?" she joked.

"No, just different. But what brought this up?" I asked.

"Erik. He calls me his white girl. I hate it." There was futility in her eyes.

"Have you told him you hate it?" I asked.

"He thinks I'm too sensitive. He doesn't even like white people that much, and there he is calling me his white girl, the thing he practically loathes," she said.

"He reminds me of my grandmother at times," I said.

"How so?"

"He doesn't give a shit what anybody thinks. You like him or you don't. He is who he is."

"Is he ever. He asks me to listen to him, even when he is silent, and I would understand him. Trouble is, he doesn't really listen to me," she said.

This took me back to my grandmother telling me about the types of women who would want to love me.

A man is his own worst enemy, my grandmother would say. *The problem with you all is that you don't listen. All you have to do is listen to a woman and you will know exactly what she wants from you.*

She had always impressed on me that I should listen, and not because it was the respectful thing to do but because it was necessary for me to guard myself.

The worst ones are those white women who will want to lie with you because of the colour of your skin, she would say. *They will love you for the experience. They will never value you.*

"He doesn't value you," I said.

"Maybe."

"Will you tell him we hung out?" I asked.

"As far as he will know, I spent New Year's Eve with my friends and that I never heard from you," she replied. "He won't question me."

She looked towards the ceiling, in a cold, empty stare.

"Erik and I, we're nothing more than what we are. He won't be taking me to Durban to meet his family."

"Do you want to?"

"I'm not going to worry about something I can't change. He told me all this from the start. I like him, but I can't change him. And he certainly doesn't want to. At some point, one of us will move on."

Chapter 7

On New Year's Day, I called my mother. The five-hour time difference situated her at home with my grandmother watching dubbed episodes of American soap operas. She and my grandmother had just returned from visiting Junior after spending the afternoon with him and the family which had taken him in.

"I place my faith in God, Salomon," my mother said to me. "Everything happens for a reason. I have to trust that he knows what he's doing."

Her faith was unshakeable. Even my grandmother whose second home was the church wasn't as fastidious in placing blind faith in God. I could hear her in the background.

"The Bible doesn't say to trust blindly. You're like that stranded sailor on the deserted island," she said. "You're dying of starvation and begging God to send you food, but every time a pig comes around, instead of slitting its throat, you say you don't eat pork. God helps those who help themselves."

I felt my mother shrug as she breathed a heavy sigh. She mentioned softly that she felt a distance between my grandmother and her, one that was never there before.

"I feel like I'm losing everybody," she said.

My grandmother did not agree with my mother's handling of Junior's situation. Left to her, Junior would never have been put out of his home. And now I sensed regret in my mother's voice.

"He's not just angry with me. He's angry with her too. Your nana had nothing to do with my decision. He ate with us, but he didn't say much, not even to her."

"He's angry and hurt, Mom," I said. "You picked Dad over him."

"Salomon, you know that's not true. You of all people can't say that to me. You know how hard that was for me. But it's temporary. I don't know why he can't see that," she said.

"That doesn't matter."

"What do you mean it doesn't matter? Your father has agreed to move in with his sister when his jaw heals."

My mother was so unaware of how badly she had mishandled this situation. I felt awful telling her the reality of Junior's plan, that he had no intention of returning.

"He's not what? Where's he going to live? Estelle and her husband can't lodge him forever."

She was incensed at the idea but justified her reasoning that he would return.

"When your father leaves, he'll come home. There's nothing out there for him," she said, as assured as she had been in her faith in God.

By the middle of February, my father had still not moved out and Junior was still living in Baie-Mahault. I was entertaining Zara and Erik in my bedroom as we celebrated Nina Simone's birthday, Erik's American celebrity crush. Apparently, she had just moved to the South of France the year before, and to Erik, she embodied the spirit of the strength and resilience of Black women. He liked her directness, saying that what others perceived as volatility was nothing more than a Black queen speaking up for herself. Nina Simone was new to Zara and me. We were in my dorm room, but I let him play the music he wanted. Watching them interact was like trying to tell the same story in two languages. There was a nuance in their interaction, a subtle chasm between their affections and their emotions. I'd be lying if I said I wasn't jealous. It wasn't the green-eyed envy type of jealousy but rather the taming of butterflies in my chest, feeling I was a better fit, while knowing this was the kind of betrayal that got men shot and kings beheaded.

The evening was well drowned in five-frankers. That was what Erik and I called wine that cost five francs. They also cost us headaches and sore bellies. So when someone knocked at the door, shouting "*Téléphone!*" on the other side, I hardly had any sense to walk down the hallway and pick it up.

"Salomon!"

It was my mother's voice on the other end.

"Boy, you drunk?"

"I've had some wine with friends, Mom," I said.

"I've had some wine with friends, Mom," she repeated, mocking me. "Boy, I send you to France to get an education and you're over there getting drunk?"

She sucked her teeth in disappointment.

"Call me tomorrow if you're interested in what I have to say. I will not speak to you when you're drunk."

I called her the next day and could hear my grandmother in the background telling my mother not to be upset with me.

"Children learn from what they see," I heard her say.

My grandmother was no doubt inferring that I had learned to drink from my father. That was a half-truth, though. I couldn't think of any island boy from my neighbourhood who didn't drink. We all drank. When the men were playing dominoes at the corner store, shooting fifty-proof rum, we were sneaking forty-litre bottles of Pélican beer right under their noses. It's a wonder they didn't catch us. But it wasn't my father—well, it wasn't just him. And it wasn't a vice I picked up in France. If anything, I learned not to answer the phone when I had been drinking.

When my mother was finally done berating me for my overindulgence in alcohol, she, like handing me a piece of iron which had been kept on an open fire since the night before, told me about my brother.

"Your brother was arrested yesterday."

She said this plainly. Her voice was dry, void of any intonation, her words flat. I was silenced by the news, shocked, as if I were burned by the hot iron and still searching for the air in my lungs to let out a scream.

"Him and four others," she said.

"For what?" I asked, finally finding my voice.

"For some debauchery in Bouillante," she answered.

Bouillante was a town on the other side of the island from where we lived in Pointe-à-Pitre.

"What was he doing all the way in Bouillante?" I asked.

"Salomon, I don't know. You young people . . . do you need a reason to do anything? The police said he and his friends were being hooligans, vandalising the place, even harassing people. Since when is that Junior? I don't understand it," she said.

She was right. That was not the Junior that I left behind just a year ago. So much had changed for him.

The charges were eventually dropped, but the damage was done. He was now known to the police. For my mother, it was the shame it brought her, that her son was a hooligan, and the guilt that it may very well have been her fault. And for the next few months, things quieted down for Junior. My mother was pleased that he started coming around the house again, although he would never sleep there. Often, he was with his girlfriend, Sandrine.

"Salomon, you know I'm still scared for that boy," my mother said to me one day over the phone.

Although she liked Sandrine, she was fearful that the girl would become pregnant.

"I won't be able to handle that. As nice as she is, she is a little simple. I could see her thinking that having a child is a good thing," said my mother.

My mother could also not get over the fact that Sandrine would confide Junior's vices to her. For one, they were both barely sixteen years old, and two, who was this girl to speak any kind of way about Junior?

"One of these days, as soon as she opens her mouth, I'll just backhand her. That child is too damn simple," my mother said.

Truth is, she would never have the guts to do such a thing.

By the end of May, I was ready to go home for the summer break. Strasbourg was great, but island life, food, water, music, and sun missed me as much as I missed them. Since Christmas I had spoken to Magalie twice; both times I was the one to reach out. Despite sleeping with me in December, she was still preoccupied with Léo, so much so that when I called her in March for her birthday, she said I didn't need to call and that December was just a moment that we shared.

"I don't regret it," she had said to me. "But I have grown from it."

I suppose it was her way of letting me down gently, not that I needed it. I wasn't hurt or insulted by it. In fact, I wondered, when I would surely see her again in Guadeloupe, if her body would still be on fire.

As for Zara, it was like we were prior to New Year's Eve. In fact, we no longer flirted. We just harboured this delicate secret between us, which neither of us wished to unravel. Even when we were alone and in private, we never discussed it, nor did we steal kisses or covert touches. On several occasions I wanted so much to sleep with her again, but I never had the nerve to intimate the desire. Most times it felt like she had just tucked me away somewhere in the back of her mind, or on a library shelf, along with the Oaths of Strasbourg, away from any reader circulation.

Interestingly, earlier that month, as the weather was getting warmer, she and Erik took a trip to Metz to see her family. I wasn't sure what that meant, except that Metz wasn't all cows and farmland. Since their trip, they had begun planning more trips for the summer, in particular to the south of the country, where they hoped to enjoy the Mediterranean. They spoke of Monaco and Italy and even Spain. They were closer, more amorous—more of everything that they both, unbeknownst to each other, confided in me that they would never be. Meanwhile, I wanted to find a reason to resent Zara—anything—like call her a cheater, but she didn't do anything that Erik hadn't done; or that she owed me something, but she didn't; or that I could stand whole in front of her, while actually I was in pieces and she couldn't see it. That New Year's Eve meant something to me, and maybe it shouldn't have, but there I was, wanting her to feel something, even if to show some semblance that she remembered, and that that night meant something to her as well.

I was getting accustomed to the cruel uncertainty of people's wishes. People never seemed to stake their wants. It was as if life just happened to them, and should it be what they wished for, then they revelled in it. Otherwise, it was just an acceptance of life happening to them. I saw this in my mother. I saw this in Zara and Erik. This made me think back to my brother's analysis of the Arab on the beach, the shooter not fully complicit in his crime until firing the second shot. I didn't want to live that way. I didn't want to love that way either. That evening, the phone rang for me one last time on the fourth floor of the Wantzenau student residence. It was my father's voice.

"Salomon, did you hear what I said?" he asked.

I could not have heard him right. Nothing made sense about that call, from him being the caller to him sharing that news with me.

"Your mother is in the hospital," he repeated. "She had a heart attack."

My heart dropped.

"She's OK. She'll be fine," he said.

"What happened?" I asked.

He appeared to not hear what I asked.

"Your nana is there with her now," he continued.

"What happened?" I asked again, a bit stern.

I felt like he was stumbling on his words, like a drunk mason at a jobsite trying to make his way over cinder blocks.

"We were just talking . . . you know," he answered.

I could feel myself wanting to go through the phone and strangle the man. But I found the wherewithal to keep my nerve.

"What were you talking about, Dad?" I asked, my words calm and measured, expecting them to be reciprocated in the same way, even though I knew they would not be.

"Look, Salomon, I just called to tell you what happened."

He paused, searching for words. I felt dismissed.

"Your nana said you're coming home the day after tomorrow?" he asked, as if he hadn't just shut me down a few seconds earlier.

"Fuck you!" I said, and I hung up.

I ran back to my room, picked up my phone card, and ran downstairs to call my brother, since the phone on my floor was only for receiving calls. Jean-Marc answered and said that his wife Estelle had taken Junior and my grandmother to the hospital to see my mother. He was expecting Estelle to call him from the hospital soon.

"Don't worry, Salomon, she'll be all right," he said.

I started crying over the phone to this man. Although he was a family friend, we were not close in any way. But I could not stop sobbing.

"How's my brother?" I asked through my sobs.

"He's all right. Does he have your number? I'll have him call you when they get in."

I gave him my phone number.

"Tell him to ask for room 412."

I hung up and slowly walked back up the four flights of stairs. My head was cloudy. I couldn't even knock on Erik's door since he and Zara had already caught the TGV down to the coast. We had said our goodbyes a few days earlier. I lay on my bed and waited for the phone to ring.

It was nearing ten o'clock, but I wished that Junior would disregard the custom of not phoning after ten. Surely this was an appropriate exception. Knowing that my neighbours would get irritated if a call came in that late, I sat by the phone in the middle of the hallway. I was prepared to wait there all night, but thankfully he called only a few minutes after ten.

"Hello . . ." I answered.

"Sal . . ."

"Junior," I said.

Knowing it was me on the other end, he started crying, sobbing like a child. Hearing his tears through the phone made me cry. I could hear Estelle consoling him, telling him not to cry, that our mother was going to heal and be back on her feet before we knew it. I don't think we had a conversation that night. Instead, we just felt what the other wanted to say. That was enough.

Chapter 8

Point-à-Pitre, June 1994

I picked up my luggage at the airport in Raizet, just outside Point-à-Pitre, and was greeted warmly by my grandmother when I exited the terminal doors. Although it was almost eight o'clock in the evening, the heat was stifling. I greeted my brother and then Estelle, who had driven them to pick me up. My brother didn't yet have his licence, and my grandmother didn't drive. Our household was always dependent on either my mother or father driving us anywhere. My father, expectedly, did not come.

It was a short drive home. When my brother and grandmother exited the car, I assumed that Junior was only going to put my luggage inside and go back with Estelle. Instead he thanked her and said goodbye. She replied that she would be back to get us at ten the next morning to visit with my mother. I was a bit surprised at it all. It then occurred to me that our car was not in the yard, and that neither was my father. My grandmother saw my face and realised what I had noticed.

"The more things change, the more they stay the same," she said.

"Where is he?" I asked.

"That's a question I'll leave for you to ask him," she answered.

Junior looked at me and shook his head. "Your father," he said, as if my father wasn't his father too, "is an asshole."

Then he picked up my bags, entered the house, and brought them to the bedroom. When he returned, he opened the fridge and poured himself a glass of water.

"Don't be afraid to offer the rest of us any, you know," said my grandmother sarcastically.

"You want water, Salomon?" he asked, looking at me.

"I'll have a glass, please," I answered.

He poured a glass for me and one for my grandmother, not bothering to ask her if she wanted any. Then he sat down at the table with us.

"What were they arguing about?" I asked.

"She won't tell you, man," Junior said. "'Ask your father' is all I've heard these past two days."

"Yes. Ask your father," my grandmother repeated. "I don't have the patience to deal with that man. Your grandfather was not perfect, and he too had his ways, but his family came first. All I can do is pray for my child right now. That's where my energy is going. I can't bury another daughter."

Mirlande was my mother's sister who had died shortly before Junior was born. She, like Junior, was an insulin-dependent diabetic. She was lean and healthy, but her pancreas did not work. It was not able to produce insulin to counter the sugars taken in her body. She suffered a stroke because of that disease. Two years later she was dead. My memories of her are vague, though I'm not sure if they are actually mine or ones that were implanted somehow through stories about her and me together.

"You all need to get some sleep. Estelle is coming early enough tomorrow. I have a feeling tomorrow will be a long day," my grandmother said.

"Nana, where is he?" I asked.

"Salomon . . ." she started.

"Never mind, Nana," I said as I got up from the table.

"He is not here. Your father's not here. Is that not evidence enough?" she asked.

"Evidence of what?"

She rose from the table, with a heavy sigh. "I will tell you children good night. Please make sure the front door is locked . . . and that Bishara girl came here a few days ago looking for you. She thought you were already back," she said. Then she went to her room and closed the door.

Junior sat there, hands up, palms open, looking at me, and said, "Don't ask me. I'm not allowed near that motherfucker, so I don't ask jack shit about his whereabouts."

"What the fuck could he have said to her?" I wondered out loud.

"I don't think the actual words matter; he's been insulting her for long enough," Junior answered.

He got up from the table and secured the front door. "We won't ask Mom anything tomorrow, though, right?"

"I'm not an idiot, Junior."

"I'm just saying . . . it was hard to see her like that. She could hardly speak to us."

"Did the doctors say anything about a release date?" I asked.

He shook his head. "I'll leave the room for you. I'll sleep in the living room. Good night."

"Good night," I answered. "Thanks."

The following day, my grandmother and Estelle accompanied my brother and me to the hospital. I felt nervous heading into my mother's room. I was scared to see her unable to do for herself. When we entered, her bed had been propped up, enabling her to sit up. As soon as her eyes caught mine, I could not hold back the tears.

"Boy, don't make me cry again. I don't think crying is good for heart attack patients," she said.

We embraced. She looked better than I had expected, and my nerves calmed down a bit.

"They're releasing me tomorrow," she said.

We were all happy to hear the news, though she didn't seem particularly happy about it.

"I don't think I'm ready to go home," she said.

"Nonsense," said my grandmother. "If the doctors say you're ready, then you're ready."

"I mean, I'm not ready to deal with home," my mother clarified.

And by home, it was clear that she meant Fritzner, my father.

"He's not in the house, Mom," I said.

"He's not?" she asked, surprised and, strangely enough, disappointed.

My mother's eyes swelled with what I could only describe as despair. She diverted her stare to my grandmother, who shook her head, confirming what I had just said.

When my mother was released the following day, she could not stop talking about everything she was seeing on the drive back. She was in the front with Estelle; my grandmother, my brother, and I were squeezed in the back seat.

"I was so scared that I would never see this place again," she said. "To God be the glory."

When we pulled into our yard, our family car was there under the shade. My father stepped out from the veranda and approached us. We rolled to a stop and no one said a word, all eyes fixed on my father. He made his way to the front passenger door where my mother was sitting and opened it.

"I've been calling the hospital for updates on your health. They told me you were being released today," my father said.

My mother did not say anything. She just took my father's outstretched hand and exited the vehicle. The rest of us did not move. I don't know what I was expecting to happen.

"Come!" my mother said, looking at us. "You too, Estelle."

My grandmother, sitting between Junior and me, shook her head. "Something is not right with this man," she said loud enough for us in the car to hear.

When we got in the house, my father already had my mother seated on one of the armchairs in the living room. I think the rest of us were still trying to suss out the situation. No one said a word, except for my mother, who seemed pleased, or rather relieved, that my father had returned. Junior did not sit down. He stood in the doorway, between the kitchen and the living room.

"Junior, come and sit down," my mother said.

He sat on the couch next to my grandmother, Estelle on the other armchair. I took a seat in the rocking chair, sitting at its very front so as not to make it rock. My father grabbed a chair out of the kitchen, placed it next to my mother, and sat down.

"How is Jean-Marc, Estelle?" asked my mother.

She wanted to hear us talk. She asked Estelle, Junior, and me about our lives, but me in particular about Strasbourg and Erik. She wanted to know more about him since I had first mentioned him in December.

"You know he's always welcome here," she said, happy that I was being exposed to the world.

I noticed her eyes fall on Junior.

"Things have a way of working themselves out. We must just put our faith in God," she said.

The midday heat from outside was starting to come through the living room. At about that same time, my mother said she was tired and needed to rest. My father sprang to his feet before any of us could and helped her to the bedroom. I heard the air-conditioning unit turn on, and then he closed the door behind him and returned to the living room.

"Jesula—" he started.

"No," my grandmother replied, cutting him off. "I'll take care of Widelene's medication. I'd appreciate it if you left the car here when you go so that Salomon can take us to where we need to go."

"Jesula, Widelene is my wife," he said, trying not to raise his voice.

"And she's my daughter," she replied in a similar tone. "I'll always protect her."

"Like you protected Mirlande?" he asked, patronising her.

My grandmother looked at him, her eyes on fire. She was never one to hold her tongue, but I could see, were it not for my mother lying ill in the bedroom, she would have unleashed a tirade of Haitian devils on him. Instead, she was soft in her speech, yet very clear in her purpose.

"After all this family has been through, Fritzner, this is where we are?"

I felt disgusted by my father. After all we had been through as a family, this is where we were, where he had brought it to. I saw a petulant child when I looked at him—even worse than a child—a wounded animal whose only desire was to claw into flesh and rip it apart.

"I'm sorry for what's happening with Widelene, but I've been dying ever since that girl died. I can't not see her face," he said.

"Well then, go finish dying, since you know so much about it," she said, and walked away to her bedroom, shutting the door behind her.

I felt like I had crashed a party to which I was clearly not invited. Estelle avoided my stare and made her way towards her purse, which was hanging on the back of a kitchen chair. As for my father, he walked out of the house, got in the car, and drove off. Estelle went to check in on my grandmother and reappeared a short while later.

"OK, boys, I have to get home. If there's anything you need, let me know. Either myself or Jean-Marc will get it for you. Right now, just keep your mother calm."

She kissed us goodbye on the cheek, as was customary, and left.

In the days that followed, my father dropped the car off in the night and like a ghost returned to his mistress. Her name was Tatiana. She was East Indian, twelve years his junior, with an eight-year-old son of her own. I had never actually seen her, until I decided one day to make the long trek to her place. Why, I don't know. I suppose I wanted to look her in the eye, make sure she was very real. After all, she had been seeing him for long enough.

So I, his older child, was standing outside their yard, not quite certain if it was indeed the right house, when the front door flew open.

Tatiana appeared at the door. There she was—very real, very tall, very dark, very Indian, very pregnant.

"Are you looking for your father?" she asked.

I was caught off guard by her directness. "Is he here?"

"He's still at work. Are you Salomon?"

"Yes."

"I'll let him know you came by looking for him," she said, and closed her front door.

I walked back towards home in the late afternoon, wondering if that was the news that sent my mother to the hospital. Is that what my grandmother wanted me to find out from my father?

Back at my yard, the Bisharas' car was there, next to ours. My mother had been having visitors since her heart attack, though none ever stayed as long as they normally would have, respecting her need for rest. I knew she wasn't fond of the Bisharas, and that was one visit she would want to curtail as early as she possibly could. I entered the house to find the pastor and his wife in my living room. I was expecting to see Magalie, but she had not come.

"Hello, Salomon," said Pastor Bishara.

I greeted him and his wife and small-talked for a bit. I could tell that my mother and grandmother were done playing hosts and that they were hoping my arrival would segue into their guests' departure. I didn't mind Pastor Bishara all that much, but his wife still irked me to no end. Her talk was so full of empty words.

"Don't be a stranger," said Mrs. Bishara. "Stop by the house one of these days. Magalie would love to see you."

Again, those were merely empty words. We all knew too well that I was the last person that Colette Bishara wanted near her daughter. Even her husband paused as the lies left her crooked mouth. But that was enough to transition them from our couch to their feet and out of our house.

Once they left I wanted to ask my grandmother about Tatiana, but my mother, now feeling better, was always there with us, wrapped up in our feet like a melee that wouldn't let us go.

"Did you guys know that Tatiana is pregnant?" I asked anyway, dropping that question like a bomb.

The two of them stopped and stared at me.

"How did you find out?" my mother asked.

"I saw her. I went there looking for him."

They stared at each other briefly, a stare that intimated their awareness of Tatiana's pregnancy.

"You talked to her?" asked my mother.

"Not really. She said he was at work and that she'd let him know I stopped by."

"Well, that will surely bring the crab out of its hole," my grandmother said.

I hurt for my mother. I hurt for the father I used to have.

"All this time I've been here, and he didn't even have the nerve to tell me," I said.

"I've been his wife for twenty years. I always expected better from Fritzner," my mother said.

We sat there, all three of us, in silence for a brief moment. "Poor man. He needs what he needs," my mother continued.

"Mom, I don't get how you can forgive him so easily," I said. "Why do you feel sorry for Dad?"

"Your father is a good man, Salomon," she said. "All men make mistakes. We all do."

"This is not new, Mom." This old news was not just old. It was wasting, rotting like fallen branches in the middle of the mangroves of the nearby town of Anse-Bertrand.

"You're right. It's not new at all. It's actually older than I wish it to be," she said.

My mother and I, though we were in the same place at the same time, were having completely different conversations. I was talking about my father's secrecy and lack of tact. She was talking about the love of her life, who was hurting and in despair, needing some healing and forgiveness, if ever he would just ask for it. It was as if she were building worlds and her hero just kept on pulling up short, but still trying his best to accomplish his mission.

My grandmother got up from the table, something obviously on her mind. She wanted to speak it, but she held it in instead. She breathed a heavy sigh, not of relief but of calm frustration. It had been a while since I actually looked at my grandmother. For the first time in a very long time, I saw her. I saw the veins in her hands and on her neck, the white of her aging eyelashes, her wrinkled lips. She had always been fierce. But right then, she was holding back something. I wondered if it was about what my father had said about her daughter Mirlande. I wondered.

"All men make mistakes," my mother had said.

This was the second time that my father had insulted my grandmother. I don't think it was a mistake.

Chapter 9

My stomach was in my throat for the rest of the afternoon and into the early evening. I was expecting to hear from my father, but I didn't know if he would call on the phone or just stop by. I wasn't quite sure what to do, so I just sat under the veranda. Shortly after, Junior came out to smoke, wearing nothing but shorts. I found this particularly interesting, as there he was, this sixteen-year-old boy who smoked and drank openly as if he were a man. And no one said anything to him. I wouldn't have dared smoke cigarettes at his age, let alone under the veranda of my mother's house. That's how much our lives had changed. Perhaps it was how far we had fallen.

I wasn't sure what he knew. When it came to my father, he didn't seem to care. He had given up. And I couldn't fault him for doing so. My father was always harder on him. Typically, it is the oldest child who suffers the brunt of any abuse or neglect, reserving the extra love and care for the last child. But my father had it backwards. Not to say he loved me more in any particular way, but there was something almost ominous in the way he was with Junior, his sharpness with him, the way he could not attach himself to that boy, as if Junior himself were to blame, as if Junior were this cactus in the middle of our living room.

"You know he's having a baby?" I asked him.

"Who?"

"Dad. His girlfriend is full-on pregnant."

He edged closer to the side of the veranda and spit. "With that Indian woman?"

"Yeah."

"You mean like nine months pregnant?"

"Could be. She's out there. Belly button popped and everything."

"Oh, you saw the bitch?" he asked, surprised.

"Yeah, I walked over there."

"What the fuck for?" he asked, spitting again. "Fuck 'em both."

"I don't really know why I even went. I don't know . . . curious. Aren't you curious at all?" I asked him.

"Fuck no. Do I look like I give a fuck? Fuck him! Fuck his Indian bitch! Fuck his half-fucking-breed fucking illegitimate fucking baby!"

He was shaking in his tirade of fucks. He put his cigarette down and went back inside, and when he returned, he had put on a T-shirt. Then he grabbed his shoes at the door and put them on, picked up his cigarette, and left. His anger at our father ran deep, and I was starting to fear that it had evolved into a burning hatred from which there was no coming back.

My brother had hardly disappeared from my sight when my father called. He was curt, with no emotion in his voice.

"Come by the house after church this Sunday," he said. "Tatiana and her boy will be away with their family for a while. We'll talk. Have your lunch first."

When he hung up, I felt my stomach churn. The anxiety I had building inside me suddenly felt like a pot of boiling rice on a hot stove, spilling over, the lid rattling, the burner hissing as the water from the pot encroached its burning surface. My hand felt numb, nearly trembling, as I hung up the phone. It wasn't fear of my father that I felt. It was the flatness of his voice, his curtness on the phone, his affair with Tatiana, his new baby. It was the reality of this talk we would have, that it would initiate the finality of my mother's desperate hope, and I would have to wear it.

My mother was up early that Sunday as she prepared the day's lunch. There was nothing better than coming home after church to a house smelling of your favourite meal. No one started cooking at twelve or at one in the afternoon, when church was over. That was the time when people reheated what they had cooked early that morning. My mother hummed as she cooked the food. In spite of the sadness she held in her heart, she was thankful to be alive. She was happy to be able to return to church and praise her God.

Church was as it always was. Pastor Bishara heaped a special praise to God for allowing my mother to return to fellowship. My mother smiled and put her hand in the air, holding on to a handkerchief and waving it as if she were surrendering her soul. The congregation cheered. In the meantime, I wondered if she was thinking at all about my father. Surely, members of the congregation knew. Were they cheering for her health or for her resilience? Or was it a cheer of pity?

Upon returning home, my mother eyed me. She and my grandmother were preparing to heat up the food so we could eat. Junior was in the living room with Sandrine, who had accompanied us to church that day.

"Boy, you need to say what's on your mind," she said. "You've been walking around here like someone gave you a stale baguette with your coffee."

My grandmother snickered.

"It's nothing, Mom. It's just been a whirlwind since getting back."

She looked at me, eyebrow raised, head tilted slightly. "You know I don't believe that for one second, right?" she asked.

My grandmother snickered again, and this time chimed in. "These children think we were born yesterday . . . like we don't know them."

"Is it that Bishara girl?" my mother asked. "I see you two didn't even speak today."

The two of them went on hypothesising on my life and my supposed sadness. I could hear Junior and Sandrine in the other room, laughing at them at my expense. Then, to the irony of my afternoon, Junior burst into the kitchen, arms wide open.

"In truth, I know not why I am sad!" he blurted out to erupting laughter from everyone.

We ate. Junior, Sandrine, and I cleared and washed the dishes. My mother and grandmother sat in the living room, my mother making crochet while my grandmother gently rocked on the rocking chair, her eyes closed. Junior and Sandrine were under the veranda. I quietly slipped away, taking a slow, mindful walk to see my father.

When I neared the house, I could see him sitting at the table on his veranda. I walked up the short cement path and proceeded up the three short steps to where he was sitting. There was a bottle of rum from the distillery where he worked and an empty shot glass on the table. He was barefoot, his eyes already bloodshot, and smoking a cigarette.

"You ate?" he asked.

"Yes," I answered.

"What you all eat?"

"A colombo."

"Your mother made it?"

"Yes."

"Is a good while since I had a good colombo. Your mother makes that so good," he said. "How's your mother doing?" he asked, after a brief pause.

"She's doing better."

He got up and went inside, and when he returned, he had another shot glass in his hand. I was still standing by the table.

"Salomon, if you're waiting on me to ask you to sit down, you'll be standing all night, you know. You and I aren't strangers," he said.

I sat down. He poured me a shot of rum.

"Your mother know you're here?" he asked, putting the bottle down after pouring another for himself.

"Nobody knows I'm here."

"You pick up smoking in France?"

"I don't smoke."

"I'm surprised," he said. "All you island boys go to the mainland and come back with a bad habit. What's yours, white women?"

He said this with a smile, but I did not smile at all. He poured himself another drink. "Do you know why you're angry?"

"We're all angry."

"Your mother is not angry. If you think she's angry, you don't know your mother," he said.

"Did she have the heart attack after you told her that your girlfriend was having your baby?" I asked.

He put his glass down and pulled long on his cigarette. He waited a few seconds before he exhaled, as if the smoke in his lungs would help him better articulate his thoughts.

"She already knew about the baby. She didn't care about that. Men have outside children all the time," he said. He poured himself another shot of rum, eyed mine, making a sign for me to drink it. "I told her I wanted to marry Tatiana."

He sounded regretful, but his regret was as nuanced as my feelings towards him. His brusqueness in saying that my mother accepted his other woman's baby bothered me. My mother loved him, but she was no pushover. She wasn't the helpless woman in the movies whose life fell apart without a man. I was trying to articulate these thoughts in my head so as to release them in a way he could understand, that my mother's pain was more than about him leaving. It had to be.

"Mom doesn't need you," I said. "But she feels like she must protect you. Her faith in God won't let her leave you."

"Faith?" he scoffed. "This isn't about faith, Salomon. This is about me . . . this family . . . this house of horrors . . . nightmares. This is me just tired."

"The only horrors I remember was you coming home drunk, insulting Nana, hating Junior, and sending Mom to the hospital."

"There's so much you don't know. Things you shouldn't know. Adult things," he said.

"I'm turning twenty. I'm not a child."

"Even so, it's not for you. I mean, your mother's and my issues are not your issues." His speech was beginning to slur.

"They affect us, actually," I said.

"They affect us all, I suppose," he echoed.

I felt like I was back in my mother's kitchen, talking to her all over again, how she seemed to be in an entirely different conversation.

"Nana will never forgive you," I said.

"Your nana can go to hell. If it wasn't for her, we wouldn't be where we are right now."

He was getting more forceful with his words.

"Your grandmother is a hypocrite," he said. "I watched that poor girl die."

"Who?" I asked.

"Mirlande, your auntie. I watched that bastard put a pillow over her face."

He sat there, shaking his head. I was looking at him, but also looking past him, trying to piece together the words coming out of his mouth. He had just ever so casually informed me that my aunt had been murdered, and that he'd seen it happen. I wasn't sure if I had heard him correctly. My heart started to race, anxious about what I had just heard.

"You wonder why I drink?" he asked, his tone suggesting the question was rhetorical.

"Who put the pillow over her face?" I asked. He was still sitting there, shaking his head, sucking back on a shot glass. "Who killed Mirlande?" I asked again.

"Robensen . . . your grandfather," he answered. "They all killed her. Well, we all did."

"What . . . who's 'we'? What do you mean?" I asked. I was so floored by the news, my words were nearly uncommunicative.

"We all watched as he did it. Your mother held her hand as if to comfort her. Your grandmother was by her bedside praying. I was just there, watching as Robensen snuffed her life away. You know, there are some things you just can't unsee."

"Why? Why did they suffocate her?" I asked.

"She had complications from her diabetes. The doctor said it was ketoacidosis. I will never forget that word for as long as I live. Ketofuckingacidosis."

Several years later I would learn the medical side of it, that her body was not able to break down the sugars in her blood, causing her to produce an excessive quantity of ketones, a chemical similar to nail-polish remover. Her blood poisoned her and caused her brain to swell, which led to a stroke.

"She was pretty much brain-dead. She didn't respond to anything," he said. "Such a beautiful girl."

"But they killed her?" I asked, astonished.

"They wanted to give her peace. The way she was, that was no way to live," he said. "The house was pretty grim for at least a year after that, until your brother Samuel was born. And six months later, the doctor tells us that diabetes is genetic and that our son, my boy, has diabetes. How do I get close to him? How do I love him? How do I wait for him to die too?"

There was a certain degree of guilt in my father's voice. Where this big Haitian man who could choke the life out of any cane was sitting across from me, there was that same man with demons and regret, telling me of this nightmare I didn't wish to know. His point had been to inform me of my grandmother's hypocrisy, but he seemed to have lost his train of thought. I wanted to press him, but he was obviously drunk. I thought of my mother, patient in the midst of all this.

My father and I sat there like salt pillars in the early evening darkness. There was no exchange. After a while, he lit another cigarette and poured himself another shot. As he poured, I finally drank the shot he had given me, as I readied myself to go home. He poured me another. Our silence was only broken by the chassis of Tatiana's car as it jumped the sidewalk onto the driveway. She and her son exited.

As she came up the three short steps to the veranda, she looked at us, disappointed.

"Better you're drunk here than at my parents'," she said.

My father ignored her. Then she looked at me, her hand over her very pregnant belly, her long hair down her back, reminding me of Zara.

"Feel free to take him with you. And don't feel obligated to bring him back," she said, and headed inside with her son.

His drunken state could not hide his embarrassment. "I promised her I would stop drinking and that I would not be a drunk, like her dead husband, Willy. As you can see I've disappointed her too."

"When is the baby due?" I asked.

"Two or three weeks . . . maybe less. She doesn't tell me anything. She didn't even want a baby. But here we are."

All this time I had wanted to think that their affair began like combustible drapes in a room full of burning candles, the drapes rolling with the wind, and at the end of their wave cracking loudly like circus whips. There would be joy in the cracking, full of passion and tenderness, their words imbued with softness, like the smell of chamomile extracted from daisies. But hearing her speak, I wondered if they were passionate at all. I could not be certain, but I felt an ebb and flow of anxiety under my tongue. A match had struck the kerosene gurgling at the base of their throat, and the drapes had caught on fire.

Chapter 10

My father met Tatiana several years ago when he and her then husband Willy worked at the same rum distillery. After an accident at the plant, her husband ended up with third-degree burns on the majority of his body. He became disabled and could no longer work, having to depend on his wife for support. A few years after the accident, Tatiana found him dead. He had hanged himself from the ceiling fan in their bedroom. His feet were not even off the bed.

"He was kneeling on the bed, slouched forward," I remember my father saying. "He hanged himself peacefully, with just enough pressure against the carotid artery for him to pass out. He didn't suffer through his hanging."

I didn't know Tatiana before then. It was only after her husband's death that I started hearing about her. I knew my father felt sorry for her. In the years prior to her husband's death, she had taken on the role of sole provider, working more than one job to support their family. Everything was on her shoulders. And when Willy finally passed, much didn't change, except for the loneliness. With the exception of her family who lived about an hour away and her young son, David, she was entirely and utterly on her own. Soon enough, my father was at her place all the time, even helping her to move from the home she shared with her husband to where she would eventually reside with her son. That was three years ago.

"Willy's death hurt me the same as Mirlande's. They were both so young. As disabled as Willy was, I saw how much his death destroyed her. She would have never wanted that for him," he said that night on the veranda.

When I returned home that Sunday night, no one was awake. The bedroom doors were all closed. I didn't imagine Sandrine was asleep in the bedroom with my brother, under my mother's very Christian roof. Then again, the way things were going, I wouldn't have been shocked at all if she were. I didn't try going in there to sleep. The earlier conversation with my father was hard, and it still didn't feel complete. There was something missing. The more I learned about my family, the more I felt there was to know about them, my father especially. I didn't know if he wanted sympathy, but I felt none to give. It was like realising I had a bad education and had to unlearn everything.

The rum was running through my veins like mercury rising in a thermometer. I was hot. I opened the large wooden windows for reprieve, then lay on the couch, grabbed a cushion, and tried not to think. Lying there, I imagined Mirlande. I pictured the words of my father. I pictured this beautiful girl. I pictured her death—my grandfather with the pillow over her face, my grandmother praying at her side, my mother holding her hand, and my father standing by. It wasn't the kind of news I wanted to hear. I wish my father had lied to me. He could have told me anything. Whether I would have believed what he said was irrelevant. I would have never imagined this. I understood their action, but the thought of it still bothered me. I felt like my sense of logic had been displaced. The same way my feelings, my love, my willingness to accept that we can do the unthinkable for the ones we love, we can also do those same unthinkable things to those very same people. Deep down, I knew, of course, what they did was out of love, that they were not murderers. They were my family, generations of strength, purpose, sacrifice. But there we were, all unravelling like a ribbon over gift paper which had suddenly been cut. I held on to the cushion and quietly cried into it. I cried so much that night that crying felt like an outer body experience, like I was watching myself cry, hoping I would just stop already. I was in a pressure cooker, and I needed someone to come in and release the valve.

Pans were crashing against one another in the kitchen the following morning. There was no need for the noise, but my mother was merciless, intent on waking me, though she pretended that the cacophony emanating from the kitchen was an everyday routine. She waited until I returned from the washroom before questioning me about the night before.

"I hear you saw your father last night," she said. Seeing my surprise, she went on. "You know the night has eyes, so don't look at me like that."

Without asking, she was wanting to know what my father and I talked about.

"Widelene, why you troubling the boy like that for, first thing in the morning? Even cock has breakfast before he crows," my grandmother said, coming out of her bedroom.

We all knew that was a lie, that the very first thing any cock does is in fact crow. But my grandmother had a way of saying things, sometimes to fit her purpose or to make a point.

"He was talking to Fritzner all hours of the night last night," my mother said, her impatience ringing through her tone.

"Oh?" my grandmother answered. "I hope you asked him the right questions."

"He told me everything, Nana," I said.

"Good," she replied.

"I mean *everything*, Nana."

My grandmother was a bit taken aback. "Everything about what?" she asked.

"Everything," I repeated.

The two women looked at each other.

"That son of a bitch," my mother said.

My grandmother was still in shock. "He did not," she said, her statement more of a question.

"Why on earth would he tell you that?" asked my mother. "What would possess a grown-ass man to tell such a thing to his son? What the hell is wrong with Fritzner?"

"Mirlande? He told you about Mirlande?" asked my grandmother, gutted.

"He did," I answered.

My grandmother's face hardened. "Papa Bon Dié," she sighed, elongating the Dié. *"Mais non."*

For the next few days, the house had an air of solemn dread. I regretted, wholeheartedly, speaking to my father. We would have all been better off had I left well enough alone. We were in late July, and I desperately wanted to see the end of August. Guadeloupe had become a tomb, where nothing grew but the measure of my will to leave, a will which was becoming stretched, a bungee cord wrapped against corner posts, hanging for life, unthreading. If memories were coins, I would have tossed them in wells and wished for more dreams, for more stories, more time on my back gazing at passing clouds, more time singing lyrics to songs I didn't know, more time ignorant of anything before my time. I had no wish to live in real life. I would have rather dreamt, stayed away from all manifestations of reality, submerged in water, cried with mermaids, fell out of planes, carried the weight of the wind between my knees—forget. But Mirlande found a permanent place under my tongue. She was caught in my throat like the rasp in my voice; she was a snare drum rattling in my chest.

"These past few days have brought up something very painful for our family," my grandmother said one evening as she sat at the kitchen table across from me. "It was painful then, as it is now. This pain is very real. It always was. But it was very necessary."

I tried to interject, but she silenced me.

"I need you to listen," she said. "You need to hear me."

She was hurting in a way I had never seen before. She felt she had to talk through that hurt to get to me, that she owed me an explanation for something I should have never been made privy to.

"Robensen loved Mirlande. He loved your mother too, but to all who could see, Mirlande was his joy. They were the same person and loved the same things, the same food, the same jokes. They talked the same, walked the same, liked the same games. People used to say that Mirlande was the son he never had, but if only they knew how much he praised God for such a daughter, they would know that no son could have interrupted that joy. He never wanted to hurt her. Left to him alone, she would still be with us. But I am the one who took care of her. I mashed her food. I fed her, wiped her face, cleaned her, did her toilet. Sometimes there were tears rolling down one side of her face. I will never truly know if they were actual tears of pain and sorrow or just her tear ducts leaking. But I knew that I couldn't see her live another day in her state."

"Nana, you don't owe me an explanation," I interjected.

"Listen!" she said, silencing me again. "For several weeks I hounded him to help me end her suffering, end my suffering too. And every time he refused. Then one day, I told him I would do it myself, that he would either come home one day or wake up one morning to a dead daughter. He was so angry with me. He threatened that if I should do anything to Mirlande that he would call the police on me. Then one day he came home from work and told me that he didn't want me to have any blood on my hands. He didn't want me to have nightmares or regret my actions and that he would help put an end to Mirlande's own nightmare. And of course, your mother overheard us talking about it. Her initial reaction was like your grandfather's, but eventually she came around."

She paused and wiped tears from her eyes. Then she grabbed my hands, her own still wet.

"When it was done, I slept in Mirlande's bed for weeks. Robensen thought I was avoiding him. I just didn't want him to know the pain her death caused me, that I cried every night, that I was having those same nightmares he wanted me not to have. After begging him to make such a sacrifice, I couldn't let him know how much it hurt me. It wouldn't have been right. On his deathbed, he asked me for forgiveness. Me? Like he had done something wrong. He had done the best thing anyone could have ever done, but still he asked *me* for forgiveness. There was nothing to forgive. I asked him to forgive me for asking that of him. I love that man. His final wish was that we be strong always for one another, to sacrifice always, and to love. Dear boy, what we did was out of love. What your mother is doing now is out of sacrifice." Her light eyes were dimming like a dying bulb.

"Thank you, Nana. Mirlande is all I've been thinking about."

"I know. I'm sorry I didn't come talk to you sooner. I asked your mother to let me talk to you. I just needed some time."

"I still don't understand Dad, and what has changed so much for him," I said.

"Your father has not changed. Your father is the same man that your mother married, the same one that your grandfather did not want her to marry," she said.

"So what does he want?"

"Mirlande's property."

"What property?"

She explained that before Mirlande's stroke, my grandfather had purchased two pieces of land for his daughters, the one where we lived, for my mother, and another, close to Estelle's, for Mirlande. After her death, my grandfather wanted to hold on to it for Junior and me. He was looking into purchasing another so that we each could have our own but fell ill and died before he could buy any.

"And you said no."

"Over my dead body. That property is for you and your brother, not for some other woman and her child."

When Tatiana had her baby a few days later, I didn't visit, nor was I invited. I was already resolved to letting my father live his life whatever way he wanted, with or without his new family. Junior did not care; neither did my grandmother. They had both washed their hands of him. My mother, however, felt sorry for him—sorry for the man he had become, for the alcoholism, the harsh words, the pain. Only she still harboured any kind of love for him, and now that I understood why, I did not reproach her.

Chapter 11

For the rest of the summer I would see my father once, in one of those moments where if I had to stake my claim to humanity, I would have refused it, evidenced that people were inherently no good. It was the middle of August, and the sky, a hue of shaded darkness, was falling. The evening light was squeezed out of it like papaya seeds thrust out of a hungry mouth. It fell all day and into the night, trees swaying in the wind, tipping their top hat to the tail end of the tropical storm that was raging miles away over Dominica. We were all at the table—my mother, my grandmother, Junior, myself, and my grandmother's brother, Yves, who had arrived a few days prior, from Haiti. Whatever devil was fiddling in malice with our archipelago outside, inside was rife with laughter, food, and music. We played cards and dominoes, listened to Uncle Yves's masterful storytelling. The Kréyòl he spoke—the Haitian Kréyòl—was different from ours. Sometimes the words were different. Other times, it was their order. But after a while, I hardly noticed. It didn't seem that different at all. I understood him all the same.

"*É Kric!*" the storyteller would begin.

"*É Krac!*" we would respond.

"*É Missié Kric!*"

"*É Missié Krac!*"

It was ceremonial, the storyteller inviting us not just to listen but to be part of his story. I had begun to enjoy these nights with Uncle Yves, listening to him dive into his tales, like sugar cubes dropped in morning coffee, the soft hissing sound of them melting in the hot liquid. His voice wrapping against his words was the silver spoon, stirring, hitting the porcelain edges of the cup. It was attention—that we should wake, that we should listen. His dreadlocks lay on his shoulders, grey and frizzled, his hands animating his words. There was majesty in him. He was regal. In another life, he could have been a king like Tenkamenin, or even the queen Yaa Asantewaa of the Ashanti Kingdom. He was a few years older than my grandmother. When she and my grandfather left Haiti, it was understood that he would stay and take care of their mother. When their mother finally passed, my mother invited him to come live with us. But when he came to Guadeloupe, he stayed only a short while, for his life was on another island.

I had begun to appreciate this man, thinking how one story, told in one voice, could affect so many, when a light passed by our kitchen window. It was too slow and horizontal in its movement to have been lightning. I hopped to the window, only to see my father rolling in, driving Tatiana's car. He barely stopped before jumping out.

"Jesula! Jesula!" he yelled, cutting an ominous figure in the torrential rain.

It was a cry we were all used to, of drunken men yelling to their wives, pleading for another chance after they had been put out.

"Jesula! You damn hypocrite! Jesula!"

And then, just like that, the drunken cry of mercy turned vile.

"I know you put some juju on me. I know you did. But you know what? No weapon formed against me will prosper. I have God on my side. You hear me? You dirty soukounian! You will rot in hell come Judgement Day."

My mother flung open the door, telling him to stop his drunken nonsense and to go home to his woman and new baby.

My grandmother came to the door. "Here I am, Fritzner. Here I am. Say your piece and get out of my yard."

"You owe me that land," he shouted.

"I owe you nothing!"

"You would rather bush overgrow on it and for it to be sucked right back into the earth than for me to have it."

"Why don't you go find the land that your father has for you?"

"Go to hell, Jesula. The whole world should know what you did. You vile people. Murder your child on Friday and back in church on Sunday."

My grandmother did not blink at the words of my father. His words didn't seem to bother her in the least.

"Call me whatever pleases you, but if I gave you my land, I'd still be a murderer. You feel the need to tell the world about what I did, go ahead. I did it and I will never regret it. So go ahead, huff and puff all you want. Blow my goddamn house down. Just know I will never sign over that land to you. Never, ever, ever. The only good thing you ever did was to father those two children. And even at that you're a failure, you pathetic excuse for a man."

"Just go home, Fritzner!" my mother said.

"Fuck you, Widelene! Fuck your mother! Fuck your children. To hell with your entire clan. I'm done with all of you."

He got back in the car. There was a loud crunch as he put the car in reverse, the gear shift pulled back so ferociously. His tires spun for several seconds on the wet, muddy gravel before he rocketed back up the hill and disappeared.

"You boys better listen to me," my grandmother said, looking at Junior and me. "If you ever wondered why that man is not good enough for your mother, now you know. If you must ever debate about whether that man is worthy of your attention, now you know. Men like Fritzner don't go away. They always come back. He will always need something and come back. Men like him are leeches. And only you can allow them to suck on you."

No one said anything. The lively raucous that was inside had been silenced. It was like a ghost had come and gone, chilling time in the process.

"I will see everybody in the morning. Good night," my grandmother said. She went to my mother's room, as she had given up her bed to her brother, and closed the door.

"That Guadeloupe rum brings the worst out of some people. I suppose you children have questions," Uncle Yves said.

"Nana already told us all about it," said Junior.

My mother and I looked at each other surprised, but relieved that we did not have to explain anything else about Mirlande.

"I don't blame her," he continued. "I would have done the same."

"I need my bed. Good night," my mother said, and went to her bedroom, closing the door behind her.

"You know your grandmother is right, right?" Uncle Yves asked us. "Fritzner will be back, even if it's with his tail between his legs."

"He better not come to me," said Junior. "I hate that man."

"I should tell you boys about this guy Hervé from my youth," Uncle Yves said as we moved to the living room.

Uncle Yves sat on the armchair, and I sat on the couch. Junior occupied the rocking chair. The wind outside was still forceful. At times it rattled the roof, and the only solace we had was knowing we were not in a hurricane. We listened attentively to Uncle Yves.

"Hervé and I grew up together. He had a baby with his soon-to-be wife, and being the womaniser that he was he got another woman pregnant. When the baby was born, his first child wasn't even a year yet. He wanted to know if the new baby was his, so he sent me to see if the child resembled him. He didn't just go on his own, knowing that the woman had been carrying the child for nine months. He sent me, me! As if anyone can look at a newborn baby and see who that baby belongs to.

"We were young men then. He was my good friend, so I went. Of course, I had very little to report. And as the years went by, he too had very little to report. He didn't take care of the child in any meaningful way. He never planned on it. He married his girlfriend. They had a daughter together. But Hervé being Hervé couldn't resist the lure of other women. He fathered another child outside of his marriage. He didn't take care of any of them. In time, he left his wife and just vanished. There was rumour of him living here in Guadeloupe, but who knows. For years I helped out his children and his wife. I started resenting him."

"Why did you feel you had to take care of them? They weren't your children," Junior said.

"No one should have to beg to live. And it was just me. I could afford it."

"So you resented him because . . ."

"Because he was a fool. Because he had these beautiful children, and he didn't take care of any of them. He had a family, and he just spit on it. But I was helping his family because I wanted to. Nothing was forcing me. So then it became so much easier to give. Then I stopped worrying about him. I no longer cared."

"Did you ever see him again," I asked.

"I didn't see him for years, until shortly after your great-grandmother died. I didn't even say hello. I just cussed him for being such a hateful man. Some of these men don't understand that not taking care of their children is hateful. It's self-hatred. I say to you, my nephews, whatever hate you have towards your father, he already feels it. He already hates himself."

"I can't not hate him," said Junior.

"I'm saying that hatred is a burden. Let that be his burden to bear."

"I hate him. I will carry that burden to my grave if I have to," said Junior.

My Uncle Yves looked at Junior, deadpan. "Don't swear upon your grave, son. Graves are forever." He stood from the armchair and partly opened the large wooden window to the falling sky, making sure to not let the wind catch it.

"Nobody respects us, Uncle Yves. I go to school with people who don't know my family is Haitian and they talk about us like we're dirt," said Junior.

"Don't you mind those people. I know many here who look at us as an example of strength. They don't look at the poverty. Why should we judge a man because he's poor, when the rich became rich by stealing from that man?"

He put his hand out the window to feel the pouring rain.

"Even the French who, under Napoleon captured our beloved revolutionary hero, Toussaint L'Ouverture, even them, who froze him to death in a prison cell at Fort Joux in France, even they have a bust of him at their prison in Besançon. Why? Because we matter. Because we have a spirit that has survived a middle passage. We have a spirit that has survived the greed of Louis XVI. It has survived slavery, famine, hurricanes. Nephew, we're still here. Don't mind these local fools who don't even know that when bombs were going off on their island ten years ago, it was Haiti that their independence-seeking brothers were emulating. Don't sell yourself short on the hatred of fools."

"They all think the worst of Haitians. Why shouldn't we hate them when they hate us because we're Haitian?" Junior asked.

"Yes, you're right. And we are Haitian. We have all the reasons in the world to hate. The French enslaved us, raped our women and daughters, auctioned us off, overworked us, cut off our limbs, took our language, tied our tongues, killed us, but here we are. They could not kill our spirit. They hated us, but we're still here."

We were listening, but Junior was still trying to make his point. Every time he felt he had an opportunity to interject, Uncle Yves just kept on talking. "It's the house's rat that eats the house. Don't let hate be a rat in your house," said Uncle Yves.

Then finally, Junior said, "It's hard when that rat looks like you."

The silence grew thick. We could have bitten into it, taken a big old chunk, rolled it over our teeth and at the back of our mouths like bubble gum, even spat it out. It was one of those palpable moments where you realise that no number of proverbs could heal a broken soul. I didn't think Uncle Yves would have had anything to say that would lessen the caustic vibration of Junior's words.

"Yes, it's painful when that enemy is our brother. But we must remind ourselves that our brother is only doing what he was taught. If our brother hates us, it's because he was taught to hate us. The white man's ways of life were never meant for us, but somehow, we inherited all of it—his ways, his school, his church, his law, his court, his justice. He forced it upon us for years, and then when he left, he left us with it, to teach it as if it was ours to teach, to preach it as if it was ours to preach, to apply a law that was unnatural to us. He condemned us by imposing his ways on us."

That was a lot of *us* being thrown around. But Uncle Yves was right. The history of the white man across the African diaspora was always the same. He comes. He dominates. He takes. And when he leaves, he never truly leaves.

"It was the devil's greatest trick," my uncle said.

"Making us hate one another?" Junior asked.

"Making us Haitians believe we were ever independent."

The rain started to drum more heavily on the galvanised roof. It was especially loud, and we all became silent, hardly able to hear each other speak. Dominica surely took a beating that night. It was the sort of beating that only the rain made us understand, for it was only after the rain that we had the clarity to see where we stood.

"Men will always want power," my uncle said. "Create a void and somebody will find a way to fill it. Create a void with a system already in place and you will find us using the same system that brutalised us, finding ways to further brutalise one another. Papa Doc Duvalier was a monster. He crippled Haiti under his dictatorship. But we can't entirely blame Papa Doc for his corrupt regime. He did what he was taught. That's why your grandmother and grandfather came here. They had to flee from Papa Doc and his goons, the Tonton Macoute."

It is a story that my grandmother alluded to often, but of which she never actually spoke. The most she did was curse the infamous Tonton Macoute, Papa Doc's secret militia, who had a penchant for dragging people and political dissidents out of their homes in the middle of the night, for them never to see daylight again.

"They came one night looking for me," Uncle Yves said. "I could see them from the fig trees. They turned the house upside down. I was feeding the pig we had in the back of the house when they came, so I just stayed hidden. I could hear them, raining slaps on your grandmother. Your mother and Mirlande were just little girls, maybe three and five years old."

"Where was Grandpa?" I asked.

"Your grandfather Robensen was there. So was my father, Gilbert."

"And you stayed hidden?"

"Yes. We knew they would come. They would have killed me."

"Why you?" asked Junior.

"I was one of many who secretly spoke out against Papa Doc. The Tonton Macoute found out."

His eyes dropped to the floor.

"Your grandmother has lived through hell," he said.

"What happened when they came, Uncle?" asked Junior.

"They held my father and Robensen down and made them watch as they raped my mother and Jesula. There was nothing anyone could do. Had I come out of hiding, they would have taken me away and killed me, like they did my father," my uncle said.

He paused, barely lifting his eyes to look at us.

"They carried my father and Robensen away. By some miracle, Robensen escaped, but my father did not. I doubt very much he lived to see the morning's light."

"Why do you tell them that story?" my grandmother asked, standing in the bedroom doorway, unable to sleep, taking us all aback by her sudden reappearance.

"They must know these things, Jesula," my uncle said.

"Their own mother doesn't know," she said.

"But why did you stay in Haiti after all that?" asked Junior.

"It rained that night, like it does now," he said.

"Worse," my grandmother interjected. "When the Tonton Macoute left, it poured worse than it is pouring now. Poor Robensen walked in soaked and bloody. I can't ever forget that night."

"Well," my uncle continued, "the rain cleaned everything. From their tyre marks to the blood outside, it just sanitised the place. I know it sounds bizarre, but I had to convince myself that I should stay."

"But why?" I asked.

"My father was missing, and my mother would not leave without him," my uncle said.

"Even if she knew he was dead?" I asked.

"When we found his body a few weeks later, there was not much left to him. We buried him, and that gave our mother some peace."

"Robensen and I had already fled to Guadeloupe by the time his body was found," my grandmother said. "But we couldn't wait. We had to flee. We had two little girls to protect."

"But if the Tonton Macoute thought that they were breaking people, they were wrong," my uncle said. "If anything, it made us want to fight more for freedom and what we believed in. That was not the Haiti that defeated the French in 1804. Duvalier's Haiti was one under the spell of a madman."

In the few weeks following that rainy night, my Uncle Yves went back to Haiti. Shortly after, I returned to Strasbourg. It had been a rough few months on the island, and I was happy to be back. Everything felt different. Indeed, everything was different. I no longer lived on the Wantzenau, as I found housing close to Kleber Square. It was also then that I decided to focus my studies on translation. Strasbourg was the perfect place for it, and the university was a stone's throw away. Much of the time I thought of how I could show the world the value of my Kréyòl language. I was preparing to pay homage to Confiant, Bernabé, and Chamoiseau, to further show the world that our Kréyòl identity was as important to us as our West Indian heritage. But that would be for later. There were other changes abloom. Zara and Erik seemed miles apart, like their trip to the Côte d'Azur had done nothing but show them that the Mediterranean Sea went on for miles, and if they chose, they too could go on forever, as they had been, while never coming anywhere close to a meaningful relationship.

It was early October when I finally said something to Erik. "Just break up with her. You don't care for her. You have these other women who give you what you want."

"I'm not giving that up. I'm the only one who's been up in there."

"Man, we're all friends. I'm friends with her too. It bothers me when you play her like that."

"Salomon, we're men. This is what we do."

"Not to our friends, man."

"Motherfucker, what's your problem? Did I say shit to you when you talked about fucking that bitch Magalie in Gwada? Man! Get the fuck outta here with that friend shit. You're my friend. She's my girlfriend. The two of you are friends by association."

He was gesticulating in a dismissive manner, not wanting to hear anything about his mistreatment of Zara. He was annoyed by my words, and though not physically aggressive, his tone intimated that I had crossed a line and that I should mind my business. And he was right. Still, there were no rules to our friendship, and too much had already changed anyway. Losing his friendship was worth me telling her that she deserved better.

"Just let her be, man."

"Fuck you! Get your own fucking girlfriend. You want her?"

"No. We're friends," I said, my voice rife with false indignation.

"I call bullshit," he said. "You think I don't see how you look at her?"

"Now you're just being an ass."

"Am I?"

"I don't look at your girlfriend. But she is my friend now, and you need to stop fucking with her," I said.

"Fuck you!" he said, and walked away from me.

He and Zara broke up shortly after. He stopped speaking to me, and since we didn't cross paths often, it didn't matter that much. Zara did not speak to me either when she would see me. I wasn't sure what I had done wrong, until I stopped her one day when she was unlocking her bike at the bike rack.

"You knew," she said to me. "You knew. All this time and you knew he was running around, sticking his dick in other women."

"I convinced him to let you be."

"To let me be what? A fool?"

"To break up with you."

"Are you stupid? You are my friend. You are supposed to tell me that he's whoring. You were supposed tell me, not some random girl in my class who he's trying to fuck."

She was right, but we were also all terribly complicated at the same time. All three of us were as right as we were wrong. We were young and foolish, full of lust and yearning, as impetuous as we felt invincible. And when we felt wronged, we hurt.

By late November, Zara and I were speaking again, going to the bookstore and the movies. We went for drinks at the breweries. There is something special about being in a place with somebody you care for—just you and that person, to laugh and talk and share, and be silent. The more we talked, the more my heart caved in. And when we kissed for the first time since New Year's Day, I knew in my soul that I would keep Zara, that she would always light my way.

"Remember that story you told me about the Oaths of Strasbourg?" I asked her one day as we sipped espressos at a sidewalk café.

"What about it?"

"I've been thinking about it. I can't seem to let go of the thought."

"What do you mean?"

"Two brothers banding together against one. Two cities. Two languages. Two countries. Makes me think of my own life, my own brothers, my destiny," I said.

"Well, you're no emperor, my dear Lothair. Junior and the baby have nothing to gain by banding together against you."

"Junior wants nothing to do with that little baby. What if he grows up thinking we're against him?"

It was all supposition. No one knew what the future held for any of us. The story of Lothair and his brothers Charles and Louis bothered me deeply, even though it wasn't anything uncommon in the history of European sovereignty.

That Christmas, I stayed in Strasbourg and visited with Zara's family in Metz. She wasn't that much different than I was. Her grandfather Aubain reminded me of my great-uncle Yves. He had stories to tell and told them with such magic in his breath. We decided that for the summer months, Zara would come spend a few weeks in Guadeloupe with me.

A few days after we returned from Metz, I received a phone call from my mother. She could hardly speak. She was trembling through the phone, her voice cracking.

"Your brother was in a car accident," she said.

I knew what was coming next. I braced myself, holding on to my breath as if it would catch me when I fell.

"He was driving Magalie and her brother."

"Driving what? He doesn't have a licence."

Silence.

"Mom! What happened?" I asked.

"Your brother will be OK," she said, and filled the air with silence once again.

"Mom, just tell me."

"They're both dead. Colette Bishara lost both of her children last night. God have mercy."

PART II

Chapter 12

Pointe-à-Pitre, December 2005

There is always a last time—when we do things, say things, go places, see people—only we never know at the time. When my Uncle Yves passed away in December 2005, I was shutting down my office for the holidays when my mother called with the news. It was no surprise, as he had been sick for some time. The last time I saw him was a month prior. He had finally listened to my mother and grandmother and moved in with them in Guadeloupe. I flew down to see him while he was still lucid, but I knew then that I would most likely never see him alive again. I want to believe that he thought so as well, for our goodbye was long. And though neither of us spoke the words, we felt it, and saw it on each other's face. When I said goodbye, I held his hands and kissed him. He had lived a full life, marred with trauma and sacrifice, but still very much full.

He was a man who had appeared so kingly to me, his dreadlocks falling on his back, thick, like a lion's mane. But that November when I last saw him, he had his dreadlocks cut off. His face was a mask that did not belong to him. Like the robe, loosely fitting his body, his skin had become a mask that didn't fit him right. It was falling off his face, not quite covering his eye sockets, his mouth crooked and drooping. Age had come for him, and it had come in the least merciful of ways. It had come as his hands trembled uncontrollably and, when most days, he forgot who we were. Neither Papa Doc nor his son Bébé Doc could dispense of him, but age did. He, who fought with the blood and strength of his ancestors, who believed in their promise that the next day would be better. Age still came for him, like it had come for them. Death was inevitable—we just never knew quite when. The last time I told him I loved him, I felt him throw his soul at me.

"The ancestors are with you," he said. "They've always been with you."

I was prepared, readied myself to not see my dear Uncle Yves again.

Sitting in the front row of the funeral service, I looked at his closed casket, and though I was there to say goodbye to my uncle, it was Magalie who invaded my thoughts. I looked over my shoulder, and there was Colette Bishara with her husband. The entire community had come to grieve my dearly departed uncle, the same way we had come to grieve Magalie and her brother. It took me sitting there at my uncle's funeral to travel back over ten years in time to when I'd had to bury my friend.

In the years since she passed, I have thought of her every day. The first time I mourned her, the entire fourth floor of the student residence on the Wantzenau came out of their dorm rooms and flooded the hallway. The phone was dangling off the hook, bouncing off the wall next to me, as I sat on the floor, crying so hard. I don't recall hearing anything around me, just seeing figures, movement, slippers in and out of doors. I don't remember how I got to my room, just that I woke up that morning and mourned her again, letting go of everything inside me. I didn't have the strength to get out of bed that morning. It was painful to breathe, my heart hurting. I thought I was going to die.

The last time I saw her was a few days before I returned to Strasbourg, when I showed up at her parents' home and sat with her on the long picnic-style table under their veranda.

"I've never been to the Alsace region," she said. "I want to visit Strasbourg."

"You should have gone there instead of Paris."

"But I love Paris."

"You're not even in Paris."

"Saint-Denis, Paris, same thing," she said.

I knew what Paris meant to her. In Pointe-à-Pitre, everybody knew who she was, especially being the preacher's daughter. Paris gave her anonymity. For me, Paris felt too big. I needed somewhere big enough to lose myself but small enough that I would not lose myself. If only I could see her again, say goodbye again, knowing that it would be the last goodbye. If only after if only after if only, no matter how many times I said it to myself or added them up, there was still not enough. If only. If only. If only. If only I could have our last conversation.

It was a conversation where we talked about her new man, this person who was as dark as me, born and raised in the suburbs of Paris. This man lay coals at the bottom of her feet, and it was clear that they were burning red, full of passion and vitality, full of desire and warmth. Léo was but a thing of the past, long gone, *aux oubliettes*, as they would say.

"What does your mother say?" I asked.

"What do you think?"

Her mother did not approve. Being from the Continent was a step up; a love interest from Europe was more desirable to people like Colette Bishara, but this man was still too blessed in melanin.

"I don't care what she says. I will be with who I want. I want to love who I want. He makes me feel like I matter. And I want to matter to him like he matters to me."

Cover me with you
Your words
Your thoughts
Cover me like you would a child
Like a blanket
Protect me

She read this, her face full of light, bright like the inflection in her words.

Cover me with your skin
Soft and naked
Tattooed with desire
Cover me with your breath
That I may breathe sighs of relief
That I'm not alone
That I'm not out in the cold

This man, whoever he was, no matter the distance, had won her over in such a way that even her mother's protestations did not matter.

Cover me with you
That I may live a little longer
That I may see one last moon
Full in her spirit, bright
A landmark for the stars.

"He wrote that for me," she said. "When I told my mother about him, she nearly fell out of her chair."

She was happy then, the last time we spoke.

Colette Bishara had lost footing where she thought she held it the most. That August storm had done more than pour over Dominica. It upset the natural order, or rather what seemed natural. And how she must feel now, knowing how she had acted towards her daughter, how she must feel knowing there is no child left to show off, how she must feel watching all the other mothers in motherhood kingdom sitting with their sons and daughters in tight brown pews at the church. I could only imagine her sorrow. Two children—gone—like the snapping of a branch, the noise lasting an instant, and then silent forever, while across the room, the person responsible for their deaths sits, greeting folks and smiling, offering them space on a pew. Yet, he offers her nothing, just an unmanageable pain that she can only stick in her gut.

Since Magalie's death, I promised myself to love better and harder, to forgive and be responsible for those who needed me. And with all that promise, I married Zara, promising her my time, my dedication, my thoughts, my words, all the love letters I could ever write. I wanted my coal to burn red at her feet, never wanted her to doubt me or wonder how much I loved her. I wanted to love her in a way that if ever my body failed, it would mean little, because we would have so much more between us. I never wished to be like Tatiana and her dead husband, or like my father and my mother. I wanted to be like the earth and the ocean, like the moon in the night sky, like hibiscus and oleander. I wanted to be forever.

We were on vacation in the Basque region of Spain when our daughter, Eliza, was conceived, presumably by the open stained-glass window in the back of the small church, tucked away along the pictorial border. That night she handed me a poem. Between us, poems to one another were love letters, but this one she insisted was just a poem.

"I wrote this for God," she said.

"So why did you give it to me?"

"Never mind," she said, trying to take it back. "You don't have to read it."

"What compelled you to write to God?" I asked, trying to keep a straight face, avoiding her reaching hands.

"So he understands my weakness and forgives my transgression in his church," she said, deadpan.

"God will not be angry," I said.

"Maybe so," she replied. "But it was a church, Salomon. Fuck. That's . . . sacrilegious. If I end up pregnant from today, that child will either be blessed or cursed."

His body is an ocean
His hands sand at my feet
Drowning will always be inevitable
My lifeless corpse
Torrid and lame
Washing up on his sandy shores

She should have known by then that nothing from her could possibly have been a curse. We were to each other what we needed. And when Eliza was born, we understood truly what a blessing was, always a love letter away from a miracle. Zara was my life. She embodied all that I felt. She was the cursive ink in my pen, a garden full of metaphors, written brightly, her prose round and full, like an expecting moon. As I sat next to her at the funeral, my mind came and went, and finally rested on her. I thought: When I die, I wish to die in her arms, and if she can't hold me, I wish to lie at her feet.

My mind travelled. It was restless under the drizzle at the internment for Uncle Yves. At the end, when Pastor Bishara came to offer his final condolences to us, Colette Bishara did not come with him. We could see her, in the distance, her hat supporting the weight of the sun. We all knew why she didn't come closer to us, and we accepted this. Colette Bishara's house was broken. It had always been broken. It was broken in the way that she looked-at-me-like-I-was-not-worthy-of-her-time broken; broken in that although we shared a skin tone, she perceived-me-as-inferior broken. It was hard to empathise with such a woman. She, who would sit in church and summon the Holy Spirit, yet her own spirit was as foul as the public latrines across the square from the church.

When I lay with Zara that night, she asked about my brother.

"I heard you tell Junior you'll see what you can do," she said. "Did he ask you for more money?"

"He needs some help, that's all," I answered.

"He's always going to need help," she said. "You don't always have to be Father, Son, and Holy Ghost. By the time we return to Strasbourg, he'll be asking for more."

She was right. By the New Year, I had already heard from Junior. Guadeloupe was a graveyard to him, a constant reminder of the tragedy of his youth, a barren landscape of island grey. He awoke to nightmares and cold sweats and my mother and grandmother leaning over him, like new mothers looking over their newborn children, wondering if they were breathing. But they did not have to wonder about Junior. If anything, they feared he may wilfully stop.

After the accident, my brother spent two years in a youth detention centre and another two years on probation. Deep down he was reeling at the thought that Colette Bishara, regardless of his disdain for her, wished him dead.

"Junior needs me. He's my brother."

"You know I will never have a problem with you helping your brother, but you need to give him legs. Help him to help himself. The Junior you talk to me about would be ashamed to be a charity case. Give him back his dignity," she said.

"I am giving him dignity. I don't want him in the streets begging and doing all sorts of dirt."

"That's not what I meant, Salomon."

"When Camille births you a brother, you will come talk to me about how I should help mine."

She turned to her side and ignored me. Maybe I should have kept her mother's name out of it and just listened to what she was trying to say. I just didn't have the patience. Her words should have been met with more tenderness. Instead, they incited riotous contempt, like tear gas thrown at a peaceful crowd.

Chapter 13

Strasbourg, March 2007

When we look at all the falling pieces, we must ask ourselves if they are falling apart or falling into place. When Eliza turned four, my mother and grandmother were visiting with us. They had been there for nearly two weeks and were getting ready to return to Guadeloupe. Junior was also there, but he had been living with us since the New Year. Zara and I agreed that he needed to be somewhere, anywhere but Guadeloupe, where he could finally forgive himself. Colette Bishara's constant gaze was upon him, and the more she looked at him, the more he looked inwards at himself in shame, oblivious to the softness that the world still had to offer him.

Around that same time, France was in the throes of what seemed a campaign of good versus evil. It was a social war worth fighting. Border security was a priority as France was supposedly, gravely threatened by immigrants who looked like me and the rest of my family. The conservative incumbent party wanted to save France, the same way Germany and Italy never needed to be saved. When you colonise the world, the world ends up at your doorstep, kind of like having children. You become a parent. You become someone's mother, their father, their guardian. You become responsible for them. You don't get to turn them away. When your baby wants milk, you put your breast in her mouth and let her feed until she's full. Then you pat her on the back until she burps, then you rock her and put her down to sleep until she wakes up hungry again looking for your breast. So, while we were all hoping that the far-right-leaning conservative centrists would fail, I took a good look at the television screen and stared at the woman leading the opposition party, understanding that barring a miracle, she and the rest of the socialists had no hope of becoming France's next president.

"You see that woman on TV, Eliza?" asked my mother. "She could be our next president."

Eliza smiled, knowing nothing that my mother said.

"You don't teach this girl these things, Zara?" she asked.

"She's a little young, Widelene," Zara answered. "No sense confusing her for the sake of education."

"Dear Lord! I feel like I'm talking to Salomon," she said. "You know how dog and owner start to look like each other after a while? It's only a matter of time for you and Salomon. First, you all start thinking the same, then speaking the same, soon no one can tell the difference by just looking at you."

I could tell that Zara's response bothered my mother. As much as she and I talked, there were certain conversations she reserved for Zara. These were conversations shaped like river stones, the ones you hold in the palm of your hand and throw over the water, watching them barely touch the surface, only to take flight, before eventually diving to the bottom. Sometimes, that stone was too smooth or too pretty to let go, and she needed Zara to pluck it out of her hand and release it.

"I wish he would find something else," said my mother in the same breath, abruptly shifting the conversation from Eliza's political education to Junior's employment. "That kind of work must attract shady people."

"Shady people are everywhere. He likes it and he's good at it," I said.

Soon after he came to live with us, Junior met a friend of mine, Raoül, who promoted artists at nightclubs across France. He offered Junior a trial run and ended up hiring him to do the same in nightclubs for the Strasbourg region. It was impossible to overlook Junior's charisma and quickness on his feet.

"You know what I mean. I don't want him getting into any kind of trouble," my mother said.

"The last thing Junior wants is trouble. I think he would walk away from any bad situation. Raoül is a good friend of mine. He's actually Eliza's godfather. Junior is in good hands."

Just then, Junior walked in. He made his way towards Eliza, a big smile on his face, and picked her up. If it were any more possible to spoil a child with love and attention, he did it. Junior was Eliza's big friend, who wore long chiffon scarves with painted nails and makeup, who had tea with all the princes and princesses of the enchanted Eliza kingdom. He was a unicorn, a dragon, a sea pirate, a burglar, a doctor, a puppy, a cat, a bed, a sofa, a mountain. He indulged her. He put her down ever so gently, as if she were a precious jewel, and sat next to her.

"What's the first thing special people like us must do before we eat?" he asked her.

"Test our blood sugar," she answered.

"That's the best answer ever," he said to a little face full of grins and smiles. "And since it's your birthday, you get to have the first finger poke."

Just the summer before, Eliza, like Junior and Mirlande, was diagnosed with juvenile diabetes. It was a hot summer, so at first as she urinated often and drank just as frequently, nothing seemed out of the ordinary. But when in the middle of the night she came dragging herself to our bed, asking for ice to soothe her thirst, we feared the worst. When the emergency doctors heard our account of events and learned of our family's medical history, they diagnosed her in what felt too quick to be accurate.

The test strip with her blood smeared over it didn't lie. When I looked back at the pictures of her that summer and saw how much weight she had lost, it baffled me that neither of us noticed that she was not well. Her ribs were stretching her skin, her sternum lying bare on her chest. Her brain had begun to swell as she had already entered ketoacidosis. When she was released from the hospital a week later, her life had changed. I never thought she would get used to poking her fingers or to receiving insulin injections. But there she was, nine months later, poking her finger and receiving insulin before having a slice of her birthday cake. Diabetes is such a heavy burden to carry, and I would have given anything to carry that burden for Eliza.

I've seen my brother give up and refuse to do what was necessary for him to manage this incurable disease. I've seen him no longer take care of himself, just so tired from not being able to just be, to just leave his house without worry, to not have to carry insulin or packs of sugar tablets or an identifying emergency bracelet. And I could see into Eliza's future. Of all the great things she would experience, she would always have this demon over her shoulder, this cloud that was anything but ephemeral, this life that could be cut more deeply than any knife could fashion. And there was Junior, the prince, the doctor, the patient, the man-eating fish, the monster, the copilot, the teacher, the student, the explorer, the uncle, making her understand that her diabetes made her special. It made him special too.

Guadeloupe was under our roof, its sun radiating with my mother and grandmother's laughter. Zara and I barely had to cook or clean or take care of Eliza since they arrived. They took pleasure in taking care of us, so indefatigably, that at times I felt guilty for it. But I never felt guilty for either of them taking care of Eliza. It was not just that they bathed her, washed her hair, fed her, and played with her but that they loved her. Their love was the cocoa butter they rubbed affectionately into her brown skin until gold flakes etched into the palms of their hands. It was the braids they silkily interwove on her head. They showed her love that only generations of women could, loving her deeply with their kindness, with their strength, with their eternal support and faithful optimism. In loving her, they passed down their love. It was like a generational book of hymns. And though they were visiting for only a short while, it was long enough to sing all the songs.

The night before my mother and grandmother's flight back to Guadeloupe, we were all in the living room. My grandmother, as always, was telling a story and segued into what was written on her plane ticket.

"Aéroport Strasbourg-Entzheim," she said. "I could never get used to these German names. Entz-heim. Can't make head from tail from that language, but I guess it found you love, eh, Salomon?"

"I can teach you," Zara answered.

"No, thank you, child," she said. "I have enough problems."

Yes, German found me love. It was because of Zara that I learned it, spoke it, and fell in love with it. It was one of the things that bonded us. I understood that in order to fall in love with her, I had to truly be in love with this city. I loved the languages upon which it was built, fought over, and by which it had nearly fallen. Strasbourg had two spirits. For all of its Frenchness, no one could deny it was also distinctively German. And Zara was this city—her—this light-skin Black girl, who's light-skin Black father married her white German mother.

The phone rang. Zara picked it up and headed to the bedroom.

"You're right, Nana. That is some kind of love. He didn't just learn German, he found a career translating it. Funny how he never translates for us when she tells him off in German," Junior joked, putting air quotes around "translates."

They laughed, but I couldn't have asked for a better career. Strasbourg was an ideal place for it. It was a hub for international relations, for students, professionals, politicians, all the elements that made translation work for me.

"And what is up with Zara?" my grandmother asked, trying to whisper. "She will either explode and take the whole house with her or just implode. You need to watch out for that girl. Is the pastry shop causing her stress?" my grandmother asked.

There was no denying that something was off with Zara. Even taking the call and heading to the bedroom was strange.

"I don't know why she would open a pastry shop," she continued. "Does she even bake? I haven't seen her touch that oven once the whole time we've been here."

"So you want her to cut the *béké's* sugarcane and come home and find some more cane to cut?" I asked.

"Salomon, don't get all huff-and-puff righteous with me. We can all see something's not right with Zara. And you yourself don't know what is going on with her," she answered. "Do you?"

"Old woman, fix your pantyhose and leave the people alone," my mother said. "You're talking about the man's wife. What is he supposed to say? What he knows or doesn't know is their business."

Although Zara started as a social worker, shortly after Eliza was born she gave it up. She said that it was not a job for the empathetic—a paradox surely, since much empathy is needed for that line of work. She described it as continually putting one's hand in a fire on purpose, because that was the only thing that could be done. Her pastry shop, La Petite Cannelle, which she owned with her friend Anouk, was only a block away from where we lived and close to Eliza's preschool. This gave her the flexibility to come and go as she needed. It was the calm that she desired—an easiness of breath without the marathon of someone else's pace.

"She worked hard for that pastry shop," I said. "It was a dream of hers for a long time."

"We all have dreams, Salomon," said my grandmother. "I just don't understand it. Where's the ambition?"

When they returned to Guadeloupe, the house was incredibly quiet. It had lost its warm Caribbean smell, and the many tastes that came with it. Eliza no longer had so many eyes on her and different sets of hands feeding her or doing her hair or reading her stories. No voices occupied the kitchen in the mornings. Coffee returned to just being coffee, baguettes just bread. Zara entered the kitchen as I was sitting at the table.

"My parents are divorcing," she said.

The news shook me. It was one of those things that you don't see coming, and then it comes and you realise it had been coming for a long time.

"Camille and Didier are divorcing?"

"Yes. I don't understand why or how," she said. "I haven't spoken to my dad about it yet, but apparently, he wants the divorce."

"I'm sorry," I said. "When did you find out?"

And then it became clear to me why she seemed so distant and bothered. Her mind was preoccupied with the fragility of her parents' circumstances.

"And you have not heard from your father?"

"I don't really want to hear from him right now."

"Did something happen between them?"

"Mom says no, but who knows. And why now? Almost forty years married, why give up now?"

"How's your mom?" I asked.

"What do you think, Salomon? After all these years married and the sacrifices she made to be with him, and just like that he wants out. How do you think she feels?"

It's not that I supported Didier wanting to divorce Camille, but I was not surprised that he would feel that way. There was an arrogance to Camille that even Zara couldn't deny.

"You're his only child, Zara. You should at least just listen first, and if you decide to be quiet after, fine. He's probably hurting too. I know I would be lonely as fuck."

She cut her eyes at me. Those were not the words she wanted to hear. I wasn't following protocol. First, I'm supposed to empathise and make it all about her. Only after am I supposed to talk sense. I broke the cardinal rule of relationships. And then, instead of shutting my mouth I only made things worse.

"I'll reach out to him," I said.

"For what?" she asked. "Don't you dare! Just leave it."

Her eyes were on fire. "I'm not kidding, Salomon. Don't you dare fucking contact him!"

"OK," I said, putting my hands up, my palms facing her.

"It's not like you can convince him not to divorce my mother," she said.

She continued her rant, as if she was addressing my responses. Only I wasn't responding. I sat there quietly, until I finally got up in annoyance and left. My leaving irritated her.

"You don't always have to be the one cleaning up the dog shit on the side of the road," she said.

"I hear you, Zara. Jesus! I said I will not call your father, OK? Only in your family do people see the dog shit and instead of picking it up, sidestep it. Maybe your dad is tired of fucking sidestepping shit."

Chapter 14

It was midafternoon on a Thursday, and except for coordinating Eliza's pickup from day care, I hadn't talked to Zara since I walked away from her earlier that morning. She had grated my nerves with her insistence on continually telling me not to call her father. Truth is, she knew me, and she wasn't wrong. We were hardly past five hours since our bust-up and I was already juggling the idea of calling her to apologise or calling her father, Didier, to get a sense of what was going on. Her insistence was an appeal to reason with me, that I wait until she was ready. She loved her parents deeply and felt trapped by her desire to protect her mother, so much so that she balanced her own feelings on a tightrope, her only safety net—me—and she must have felt like I wasn't there.

I decided not to call either of them. I was certain she would be preoccupied anyway with Anouk, renovating the back room of La Petite Cannelle. The sales area was fine, but in the back was their kitchen, where they did their own baking, and a small but cozy living space. They had it set up for their lunch break, or when they needed to rest after work, with a couch, table, microwave. It was theirs and only when invited could anyone enter. Between the baking, the sales, and the renovations, her hands were as engrossed as the belly of a full moon.

As for me, I would spend the rest of the afternoon looking through résumés, trying to expand my translation business. Whenever I thought that maybe I should wait, cut back on my ambition, opportunities kept presenting themselves. At the end of the day, it was not solely for me.

I wanted my mother and grandmother to be cared for in the best way possible. I thought of my grandmother especially. I didn't want what happened to Uncle Yves to happen to her. He had to leave behind everything and everyone he knew in Haiti and move to Guadeloupe to be looked after and cared for, yet he only got sicker and died. I didn't want that for my grandmother. I wanted to be able to afford the care nurses who would come to the house more often than the weekly mandated visit by the health authority. I wanted her to stay in her home. Most of all, if ever she was ill, I wanted to be able to visit and stay for as long as I needed. I also did this for Eliza, to give her a step up in what I didn't have, an opportunity to not need to struggle. And lastly, as it goes without saying, I did this for Zara, my life partner. I did all this for them—all of them.

"I'm sorry," I said, when I walked in that evening.

"Careful where you walk," she said. "Don't want you stepping in shit."

"I'm trying to apologise," I said.

"My parents are getting divorced, Salomon—my parents—mine. What good is an apology to me? It might make you feel better, but it does nothing for me. You didn't have to be so insensitive. That's my only family. I don't get to go back *home*. My dad wouldn't know the first thing about Guiana if it hit him in the face. I don't know my family over the river either. You know why. Do you really want to talk about people who are sidestepping shit? Really?"

She planted her metal stake in the dirt, marking her territory as she eyeballed me, signalling that I should not cross it. I could feel her eyes cutting me with her glances. I felt her disappointment, deep like her patience was short, bouncing off the kitchen countertops, her body language intimating an anger emanating from the soles of her feet and rising, the red of the heat radiating from her chest into her throat. I said nothing else.

She left the kitchen and went into the living room and sat on our couch. I watched her from the kitchen. When she noticed me looking at her, she stood up from the couch and headed towards the bedroom.

In the still-dark early hours of that morning, I woke up to an empty bed. I assumed she had gone to sleep with Eliza, which she did on occasion when she was upset with me or if she had fallen asleep while putting our daughter to bed. I lay there, unable to fall back asleep, and then was suddenly hit with the irrational fear that she may actually not be home. I jumped out of the bed, panic stricken, and made my way in the dark to Eliza's bedroom. When I got to the dining room table, a dim light from Eliza's room was glimmering onto the couch. It was that visual for some reason that made me stop, and I sensed my irrationality. I felt I should return to bed, but instead I stayed the course and approached Eliza's doorway. I found Zara on her feet, looking out the window. She turned to me.

"Your daughter is hard to sleep with. What's your excuse?" she asked.

"Just wondering where you were," I answered.

"So you sent the search party?"

Feeling awkward and foolish for going to check on her, I started walking back to my bed.

"We're better than this, you and me," she said.

"Yes, we are," I said, stopping to look back at her.

"I accept your apology."

"Come back to bed," I said, extending my hand to her. "We can talk about all this tomorrow."

I pulled her into me and embraced her tightly. No matter our issues, she was the woman I loved, the person I trusted most in the world, the one whose soul mirrored mine, the mother of my child. In that early-morning hour, I wanted to consume all of her, to take all her power, her femininity. I wanted it all, the same way a raging wildfire consumes dried bush. I cupped her face in my hands and kissed her lips, feeling myself grow against her body. We kissed, at first gently, and then more ferociously, our fondling turning to groping.

"Not here," she said, ushering me out of Eliza's bedroom.

Closing Eliza's door was the permission we needed to be our tribal selves, to sweat, to want, to need, to take, to give, without any reservation. The darkness felt bright, our nakedness the colour of the earth. We never made it to our bedroom. Instead, we found each other in the middle of our living room, against the blue hue of the couch, wet with sweat, like damp laundry laid out to dry. It was a knee-buckling kind of feeling, an overture of peace and hope and deference.

The following morning I went to work early, leaving Zara and Eliza having breakfast at the kitchen table. When I got to the office, Margaux, who worked on the French-Russian translation team, was already there. She was the only Afro-Russian I had known in all my life. Besides her roots, I knew very little about her. In subsequent conversations I would learn that there were many Russians of African descent living in Russia. They were mainly skilled Black Americans who wanted to escape the brutalities of a Jim Crow America and were welcomed in Russia. She was not of that heritage, though. Her Russian mother married a Black French man. Margaux was atypical in her look, opting not only to cutting off her hair but shaving her head.

She was removing stacks of paper from their cardboard boxes and then tearing the boxes down. She was a go-getter, always taking care of things. I wasn't surprised to see her in heels breaking down boxes.

"Good morning, Margaux," I said.

"Good morning."

"Great minds think alike?" I asked.

She was never at work this early, usually arriving a good forty-five minutes after me, and I was myself already half an hour early. She gave a quasi smile and continued tearing down the boxes.

"That's why I hired Alex, you know," I said. "He delivered the boxes late yesterday and had to be somewhere, so he left them unpacked. But he said he'd be back this morning."

"Well then, he'll have a bright start to his Friday," she said. "Actually, I'd like to talk to you about my schedule when you get a chance."

"We can talk now. What is it about your schedule?"

"Lucas and I are divorcing," she said.

She was very matter-of-fact, contrasting our initial pleasantry with a dry brusqueness.

"We have separated, but we've worked out the boys' access between us, for now anyway," she continued.

"I am very sorry to hear about you and Lucas," I said.

"On days I have the boys, I have to leave here by two thirty. I can make up that time by coming in early on mornings, like today, or staying later on days I don't have them," she said.

In the six years since Margaux started working for me, she had gotten engaged, married, had children, and now was getting divorced. I met her husband a handful of times, but not enough to make any fair assessment of him. We did nothing together outside of work hours. To hear that she had difficulties at home was shocking but not, in the sense that I knew nothing much of her personal life. What I knew was that she was always well put together and professional, hardly ever absent. She was the ideal employee, dependable, someone I respected. Six years is not a long time, though it could be a lifetime. Her twins were under two years old. Before their separation, her husband was able to pick up the boys from their childcare, allowing Margaux time to get home later.

"Take whatever time you need. I won't micromanage your schedule. Do what you need to do," I said.

"Thank you, Salomon," she said. "Your understanding means a great deal to me."

"I wish I had known you were having a hard time."

We were strangers in the sort of marriage that served its purpose, where what needed to get done got done, and what needed to be said was said. All the affective part of it did not exist. If this were love, it was an arranged love, built solely on each other's need and not based whatsoever on desire or want. In those six years, I never truly saw Margaux. Maybe she brought her bad days to work, maybe she wiped her divorce on her blazer's sleeve. Maybe she breastfed at the conference table. Maybe she knew much more about me than she let on. I couldn't say the same.

That night, as Zara and I were lying in bed, I brought up Margaux, and how I felt I didn't know anything about her life.

"You can't know everything about all your employees," she said.

"I don't know anything about any of them."

"That's not your job. Their personal life is not your business."

"You and Anouk are friends," I said.

"That's different. Anouk and I were friends before opening La Petite Cannelle. We're business partners. She's not my employee. Why are you bothered that you don't know about her life? Are you going to know all your employees now?"

"It's not that. In my mind, we were friends. And now, it's clear that we're . . . not."

She turned over dismissively, assuming a foetal position, no longer wanting to entertain any thoughts of Margaux. "Well, right now it's clear that I'm going to bed. I have no interest in talking about the other woman in your life."

Midway through the following week, I stayed later at work. I had become obsessed with the Oaths of Strasbourg and wanted to translate them into Kréyòl, but not any Kréyòl, Haitian Kréyòl—the Kréyòl of my ancestry. The more I learned about the Oaths of Strasbourg, and how they were pronounced and to whom, and of the speeches that were made by the kings, the more I was drawn to the document. Though nothing had yet happened between me and my brothers, something about the oaths mirrored my life.

The custodian, Alima, had just indicated that she was done for the evening and said good night. Soon after, there was a gentle knock on my office door as Margaux, also working late, peeped in.

"Proofreading?" she asked.

"Among other things," I said, looking up.

"I know that feeling much too well. When final edits fall on your shoulders. That's why I give my team early deadlines."

"Oh, I've heard some grumblings," I said.

"Who have you heard grumbling?"

"I'm not saying a word. Funny thing is, they speak openly in my presence, as if I wasn't even there. I swear some think you're their employer."

"I did interview and hire some of them, so quite possibly." She chuckled.

"You ever thought of going out on your own?"

"Lucas wanted me to. But he doesn't understand what it takes to build a strong translating team. I'm not ready for that."

"Well, good thing you didn't listen to Lucas. We'd miss you around here," I said. "How is everything going? It must be quite the change."

"I never thought I would be a divorcée. But here I am. And frankly it is for the better. It's been a long time coming."

"It's not easy is it, marriage?" I asked.

"Well, I think my experience makes me a bit biased. I should be asking you," she answered.

"I think the question was rhetorical," I said. "And yes, we're all biased."

She took a deep breath and nodded. There was a silent acknowledgement that other people's private relationships are not necessarily what we think they are, and for the first time, I saw beyond Margaux's professional veil.

"Can I admit something to you?" I asked.

"Sure."

"When you said you were divorcing Lucas, I was shocked, partly because I had no idea that you were going through anything. But also because, in all this time, I thought we were friends, only to realise friends know each other. They know about their lives, their weekends, about each other's struggles."

"Sometimes that's not a bad thing, not knowing," she said. "There are certainly pros and cons. I mean, you didn't tell me about Zara doing that pastry shop venture. It was all by chance that I stopped in there one day and discovered it. I buy from La Petite Cannelle often. Zara doesn't even recognise me, and I don't bring it up. Maybe it's because I shaved my head since I last actually had a conversation with her. In any case, I feel it's easier to walk in there, make my purchase, and leave."

"But had we talked about it, had you mentioned you stopped there, that you talked to Zara, it would have been one less wall between us," I said.

"Are you going through some early midlife crisis?" she joked.

"No, no crisis."

We paused, smiling in appreciation of the moment. It was funny, but it was also tender. There was something connective about it, like us finally seeing each other for the first time.

"I'll just make it a point to know the people around me better from now on," I said.

"I'm sure you have a lot on your plate. But yes, these days, I could certainly use a friend."

My conversations with Margaux made me consider Zara's parents. I wondered what the matter was with Didier and Camille's marriage, truly. Was it an absence of being seen? Or heard? Appreciated? I had to respect Zara's decision not to reach out to her father, but the desire to call burned just as much as wanting an answer to why he no longer wished to be married to Camille.

That Friday afternoon, Didier called my phone while I was still at work. "I'm in the city for the weekend. I'm staying at the Esplanade Hotel. Can you meet me?" he asked.

I left work early and walked the few blocks to his hotel. I didn't say anything to Zara. He met me outside and we walked to the brewery, on the way passing some of the university buildings.

"I can't recall the last time I walked through here," he said. "Back when it was Université de Strasbourg. Now it's Université Marc Bloch. Typical white people, always renaming buildings after their white heroes."

I didn't say anything. I knew Marc Bloch fought in both world wars and was executed for being part of the French Resistance. Yes, he was white.

"You and your silence," he said. "The immovable mountain that is Salomon."

"I'm just listening to you," I said.

"And that's the problem. Always listening. All we do is listen. Black men have listened ever since they came off these ships from Africa. Listen. Listen. Listen. What have you heard, Salomon, from all this listening?"

"What's on your mind, Didier? What's going on?" I asked.

"I like how you are with my daughter." He stopped and faced me, removed his hat, and passed his hand through it as if he were cleaning it. "I like how you take her back home to your family, how you ground her in her Blackness."

He put his hat back on.

"I could never give her something I never had myself. It's through you I realise what I don't have—what my father never gave me. I so wish I had that connection to somewhere else than here. The only Blackness I have is the colour of my skin, and that's not saying much. My father came to this country and never looked back. He never talked about his past life. He raised me and my sister as the little mixed-race children that we were. He just left out the Guianese."

Whenever Zara spoke of her Guianese grandfather, she spoke proudly of him, his Africanness always a focal point in her representation of him. Her father was describing a much different person.

When we arrived at the brewery and sat down, I said, "She's not taking your call because she's not ready to be disappointed by one of her parents."

"I know I'm on the wrong side of this one, but in the end it will be better for all of us. Sounds cliché, right? But it will liberate us all. Especially Zara. I know she'll come around."

"What happened with you and Camille?" I asked.

"What happened between me and Camille happened way before me and Camille," he said. "Ever heard of Léon-Gontran Damas?"

"Guianese poet. Author of 'Hiccups.'"

"Do you recall the ending of that poem?" he asked.

"Something about no banjo or guitar, just violin," I said.

"And that has been my life," he said. "Imagine a Black man living his entire life on the periphery of his own Blackness. I'm almost sixty years old and that's all I've known. It's time I find my way home."

"What about Camille?"

"I never asked for a divorce. I don't want a divorce. Camille doesn't listen to understand what she doesn't understand. I only told her, if I was to marry again, I wouldn't marry a white woman."

He must have seen my eyes open as if I were trying to find my way in the dark.

"You told your white wife of thirty-plus years that if you were to do this again, it wouldn't be with her?"

"Sounds worse than it is," he said.

I was listening to this man trying to justify what I thought was not just ill-contrived wickedness, but lunacy.

"I was trying to explain to her where I am on this journey that I'm on," he said. "It's my self-rediscovery. It's not about her being white. It's about the Blackness, and Black people, and my responsibility to the Black woman. They're always at the bottom of the barrel. Nobody is lifting them up. It's hindsight, what I would have done to educate myself better. I would have found my way home and not wait on my father to take me there. I'm not looking to remarry."

It was inconceivable to him that Camille would be offended by those words, and maybe he was right. I understood, but were it me, those words would have stayed locked away in a vault.

"That's what I want to explain to Zara, and maybe she can explain it to her mother, because I'm not getting anywhere. All Camille's hearing is accusations that she's white and that I don't want to be married to her anymore. I even asked her to come to Guiana with me, but she said it's something I should do on my own. I've never done anything on my own. Never done anything without her."

When I got home, I explained to Zara what had happened, that he had called, and we had met and talked. I tried offering details about the conversation, but she wanted none. She went to sit on the couch next to Junior. I sat across from them. It was then that Junior informed us of his dissatisfaction with his job.

"The money is good, but that lifestyle is not for me," he said. "It was exciting in the beginning, though."

"You were broke in the beginning. So yeah, getting paid would be exciting," I said.

"I can't do this for the rest of my life."

"You want to quit?" Zara asked him.

"I'm looking for something better. I'm considering going back to school too."

"It's only been three months," she said.

"Feels like a year. I don't like that kind of stress," he said.

"Well, don't just quit on Raoül," she said. "He gave you a chance."

"Raoül is a businessman. It's all about the money. If I didn't make him money, he wouldn't have kept me. I don't owe him anything. I make money for that motherfucker. I die today, he replaces me tomorrow."

Junior sat there, the dreads on his head beginning to take shape like a crown, a yellow, green, and red bracelet around his wrist. He was in direct contrast to Didier, sharing space with the person whom Didier only wished would return his call.

"I've been looking for my own place," he said. "I don't want to overstay my welcome."

"You're not a bother to anyone here. I mean, go if you want to go, but no one is pushing you out," she said. "Stay until the summer and save some money."

"It's time I go."

Zara got up, sighed, and walked towards our bedroom.

"Everybody just up and leaving, quitting on everybody. Four months, forty years, it doesn't really matter," she said. "Whatever happened to loyalty?"

Chapter 15

With the presidential election on the horizon, I was anxious about a conservative presidency. No matter what gains we made as a society, it always felt as if it could all be taken away by the stroke of a pen. Life moved on, but there was a hesitancy in the air, a sort of anxiety, like darkness brooding at the sight of daylight.

It was a Saturday in the beginning of April, and Junior was in the midst of moving out, making trips back and forth to his new apartment. Zara was at La Petite Cannelle, leaving just Eliza and me in the house. Eliza would be starting kindergarten in the fall and was already excited at the prospect of being in the big school. She was growing. This beautiful thought, conceived in my mind that I should love forever, teach her, protect her, show her the way through this maze of unpredictability, was now more than just a thought. She was alive, a beating heart and soul, with ten fingers and ten toes, two ears, a mouth, a nose, with thoughts of her own, with words, with feelings, with love. She may have been her mother's heart, but she was my life, my greatest joy. I would have done anything for her. Other parents may qualify that with "within reason," but to me, she was reason enough.

Between Junior's trips he stopped to have lunch as Eliza was playing in the living room. "You ever think of Magalie and Clément?" he asked me.

I was shocked by the question. In ten years, he had never brought up the accident. "All the time."

"It's weird, but it's Colette Bishara I think of most, and how lonely she must be. I never liked the woman, but if I could give her back her children I would."

"She must be lonely. Nana said that Pastor Bishara has been in and out of the hospital. No one knows what is wrong with him," I said.

"If anything happens to that man, she'll kill herself."

"You know there are services to help you deal with whatever you're feeling."

"I don't need help with my feelings."

"It's to help you process the pain."

He shook his head, biting into his sandwich. "If Dad died, would you go to his funeral?" he asked.

"Of course."

"Why?"

"Because he's my father. And Mom would go. So would Nana. We would expect you to be there."

"Never happen."

"Well, he's not dead yet, so all's moot at this point."

There was something more he wanted to say, but I felt that he wanted me to ask, as if it were a Pandora's box and he didn't want to be responsible for what came out.

"Where is he even living?" he asked.

"Last I heard, in Capesterre with some woman."

"And Tatiana? What about the boy?"

"I help her out here and there."

"Still doing that shit?"

I'd expected that reaction from Junior. But Mehdi was my brother too—our brother. I wanted to get through to Junior that we could not punish the child for the actions of our father.

"He's our brother."

"Not my fucking brother," he said, his tone harsh and intimating finality. But then he posed a question. "Anyway," he said, moving on from Mehdi, "let me ask you this, now that you're married and have a child of your own. You ever wonder what kind of love they had, Mom and Dad?"

"I used to struggle with it. I used to say I didn't know what kind of love it was. But I knew."

"Well . . ."

"Adulterated, passion-less, patience-less, sex-less, touch-less."

As I said the words out loud, I had this bad taste in my mouth, like what I always imagined stale bread soaking in water would taste like, churning my stomach.

"No-time-for-you love, we-should-never-have-gotten-married love, we're-better-off-divorced love," I continued.

"I-hate-myself-for-loving-you kind of love," he said.

When he said that, I wondered if this was really about my mother, or if it was just Junior projecting his self-loathing. He seemed to have his life back on track, but under the surface I had to wonder, knowing that sometimes even on the darkest night, we find ourselves looking for shade.

"How did she ever marry him? I mean, she must have known he was an asshole," he said. "I don't like the man, but at the same time I don't understand these women who marry men like him."

Junior was incensed. There was something about the way men like my father got involved with good women that bothered him. He felt that these women paid a price that should never have been.

"Even Zara's dad, now he wants to be all militant and Black? If I was Camille, I'd drown him in the fucking river. How is she supposed to feel?"

"Zara and Didier are talking again. They're figuring out their shit. It's like the mud after the rain."

"Yes, men are always raining. Rain, rain, rain."

About a month later, Zara and I watched the new French president get elected. It was clear that our socialist ideals threatened the French Republic, and as a result the pendulum swung further in favour of a conservative tide. Anything other than conservative would not do. It was us, feeling left out of a conversation, not because we had nothing to say, but because no one cared enough to even pretend to listen. I thought often of what Didier said to me about listening and whether I'd heard anything. Well, we heard enough that night. We heard the refugees banging on the gate. We heard them wailing to be let in, only for hot grease to be poured on them from an upstairs window.

"He looks like a crook," Zara said of the new president. "I predict a scandal over the next five years."

"The sad part of all this is that he was actually voted in."

"Dad will be so upset," she said. "That's why I want to take him to Guiana this July."

"Your mom too?"

"She doesn't want to come. She's still upset."

When July came, Camille and I accompanied Zara and Didier to the airport. Camille was nothing like I expected. She was happy and excited to see them off. The entire car drive back home she was fine. When we finally parked in the driveway, there was a solemn sense to her, like she had received bad news and she had no choice but to mourn it then and there.

"He's not coming back to me," she said.

"Zara is bringing him back."

"There is no bond stronger than those two. I learned a long time ago not to compete with her father's love. And they share something I can never be a part of."

She unbuckled her seat belt and twisted her body to face me as I turned off the engine. We were quiet for a moment. I didn't quite know what to say.

"I wish you had gone with them. You're seeing this the wrong way," I said.

"There is no wrong way to see this unless you're blind. *Didier ne me voit plus. Il ne voit qu'une femme blanche.*"

"That's not true. He sees you. He sees more than just a white woman."

I kept denying out loud what she was saying, until my words no longer mattered. I would just shake my head in silence again, and again and again.

Zara and Didier were gone for ten days. Camille did not return to Metz right away. She stayed a few days with Eliza and me. She suggested that she and I do something together, just the two of us. I agreed, though I was not altogether ready for what she had in mind. When the day came we drove about thirty minutes outside of Strasbourg to the Vosges Mountains. We arrived at a sign which read **NATZWEILER-STRUTHOF**. It was a museum of what used to be a concentration camp.

"This is my second time here," she said. "You may hear many of us say that there were no death camps in France, but this is the exception. This is the only one, as far as I know anyway."

There is something very sombre about visiting a Nazi concentration camp. I didn't even see the need to have signage about prohibiting photographs. I felt no need to take pictures. The atmosphere was immemorial enough.

"This reminds me of a story my great-uncle told me about Toussaint L'Ouverture, who, after his rebellion was kept in prison without any blankets in the middle of winter, right here on French soil. To think how a man can freeze to death at the hands of other men," I said.

"Men do terrible things. They've always done so and will not stop. I have family who died here, German family who crossed the Rhine and settled in Strasbourg, in Metz, and the surrounding areas. People who became members of the French Resistance. People who just vanished into the 'night and fog,' as they called it."

Camille was transported back in time, lost in the moment.

"I was born in 1953, Salomon. These camps were shut down only in 1945. That's not even ten years before my birth. When we celebrate VE Day, my family is not celebrating. We are mourning all over again—mourning our family, our friends and neighbours. And I take nothing away from the soldiers who gave their lives and the millions of Jews who perished in places like these, but for me and my family, we lost our own people fighting as part of the Resistance."

We made our way down a gravel path which led to the gas chambers. Hardly anyone around us was talking, and those who were talked so softly that I heard the crunch of the gravel under my feet, the sound we make when shovelling sand into a bucket.

"I don't talk to many of my family now. Zara has never met my mother. To think we can go through such horrible and despicable trauma, trying our best to beat hate, but still we get caught up on the colour of a man's skin. I love Didier, and I chose him over my family. And now, I feel so betrayed by him. I would honestly have preferred he slept with another woman. That, I could get over."

She spoke this truth with such melancholy, yet still managing to talk softly enough, only for me to hear.

"I'm no idiot, Salomon. I understand the principle behind Didier's awareness of his culture."

"So why didn't you just go with them?"

"I met Didier in 1974, here of all places. I was twenty-one years old. He said hi to me in the parking lot, his big brown eyes looking at me, as if he was looking for something more than just a 'hi' back."

She was transported again. This time, though, there was steel in her voice.

"And then he said hello again, right down here by one of those chambers, can't be sure of which one. As sombre as this place is and was back then, my heart exploded. So why didn't I go? Because over the next few years, we were inseparable. And when I told him that my family would no longer be in our lives, there was no explanation needed and we never talked about it again. It was a fait accompli."

She could tell that I was still looking for an actual answer. Her words and her demeanour did not match. I felt confused.

"If you had to cut your mother or grandmother out of your life, you'd understand it's not as easy as it sounds. I miss them sometimes.

He could have suffered in silence too, the way that I have suffered. He could have kept it in. He didn't have to say those things to me. There was no need to hurt me like that. We all have our burdens."

She returned to Metz the following day, leaving me with Eliza and planning to return only when Zara and Didier did. I tried to explain to my mother what had happened, over the telephone.

"That woman doesn't know her ass from her elbow," shouted my grandmother in the background. "How is she supposed to know anything about a Black husband?"

My mother tried shushing her.

"Pass me that phone! Let me talk to that boy!"

There was a muffled silence as I imagined her making her way to the phone.

"Salomon?"

"Yes, Nana."

"Don't you mind that woman! Don't get involved in any issue between her and her husband and her child. When things go wrong, they're gonna point the finger at you."

My mother got back on the phone.

"She's right, you know, Salomon."

"He knows I'm right," my grandmother shouted. "You don't have to tell him I'm right."

As we finished our conversation, I told my mother about my intention to have a party for Junior's upcoming birthday in the fall and that I wanted the two of them there.

"She doesn't do too well on those long flights, you know. We'll see," my mother said. "Before I forget, Pastor Bishara was admitted to the hospital again the other night. We're all praying he's out again soon."

When Zara and Didier returned, they were red with sunburn, like amateur tourists. Didier held Camille and embraced her as if she were long-lost family. There was regret in his eyes, and sorrow. Zara watched them, herself tearing up. They left the airport and headed straight back to Metz. Zara, Eliza, and I headed home, where Zara's jet-lagged body succumbed to fatigue on our bed. She was still sleeping in the late afternoon when my mother called.

"Pastor Bishara died this morning. Poor man never left the hospital again. I don't know what Colette is going to do with herself."

Chapter 16

It was raining that Friday morning when Junior and I drove to the airport to pick up my mother and grandmother. Junior had no idea they were coming specifically for his birthday, which we were celebrating the next day. Camille and Didier had driven down from Metz and had been with us since the middle of the week. In the meanwhile, we were going to have a very full house.

The overnight flight from Guadeloupe to Paris was on time, but the flight from Paris to Strasbourg was behind schedule. Junior and I waited at the airport bar.

"You think Nana will say something about white people and piss off Camille?" he asked.

We sat there and laughed, reminiscing about our grandmother's actions and words. We acknowledged how much anxiety she gave us at times when we were not sure how she would react in certain situations. She was the most direct person either of us had ever met. She didn't care what the world thought about her.

When my mother and grandmother eventually disembarked, I first saw my mother's sun-kissed face. It was darker near her eyes, especially around her temples. She grinned wide, exposing her gold caps, as we embraced.

"When did I birth two grown men?" she asked.

"Where is Eliza?" asked my grandmother. "You know the only reason I put up with this flight is for her. When she's old enough to travel by herself she will come spend her summer vacations with me. Until then I will have to suffer these eight hours of flying."

"Woman, the plane has hardly landed and you already starting trouble?" asked my mother.

My grandmother looked over at my mother and sucked her teeth. Our reunion felt as if we had not been separated for the last six months. We were back to our stories and teasing and jokes. It was like we had just gotten back home from a day's work.

As we neared the house, I informed them of our sleeping arrangements, that they would have our bedroom since Zara's parents were in the spare.

"I suppose Camille will want to do some cooking," said my grandmother.

On the periphery of my vision I could see my mother rolling her eyes.

"And I'm supposed to eat it, huh?" asked my grandmother.

"Mom, what are you trying to start with Camille? Don't embarrass the boy with any nonsense. Just eat the food," said my mother.

"Well, you make sure she knows I don't eat cornichons and ham."

We laughed.

"Nana, nobody is feeding you pickles and ham for lunch," I said.

"How long are they staying, Salomon?" asked my mother.

"They're leaving on Sunday."

"So, we have three days to survive Camille and Didier Archer," said my grandmother.

"You mean, three days to survive Jesula and Camille," said my mother.

I parked and we sat in the driveway, looking at the house. We could see through the kitchen window, Camille looking back at us.

"You see that . . ." said my grandmother. "See why I don't trust that woman? She's starting with me."

"Jesus, Mary, Joseph! Just three days, God. Please give me strength for three days," said my mother.

The side door to the house opened and Camille came out, followed by Didier. We exited the car and the four of them greeted one another warmly, among them my grandmother, who, to no shock to my mother, Junior, and me, told Camille that they must stop meeting in this cold place and offered that she and Didier come down to Guadeloupe for some cane rum and coconut water for their palates, hot sand under their feet, and most of all, some unforgiving sun on their faces.

By the time Zara came home with Eliza, Junior was already gone.

"Who did he say he had dinner plans with?" asked my grandmother.

"You'll have to ask Junior next time you see him, Nana. I'm not getting into his business," I said.

"It's my friend Anouk," said Zara. "She co-owns the pastry shop with me."

"That's not good," said Camille. "You're all friends. If things go sideways, somebody will be miserable. Salomon, you couldn't counsel the boy?"

"It's not like Zara counselled her friend," said my grandmother.

"Let us slow down here as far as who needed to counsel who," said Zara. "These two people are adults. The so-called *boy* is turning twenty-eight tomorrow. It's not my place to get in his business."

"A little too late for that," I said.

"Regardless, there is a fine line between work and home," said Camille, "and we should keep those very separate. The most dependable thing about people is that they will reveal who they truly are, when they are hurt or angry, mainly because they're spiteful."

"Well, for now they're having dinner. Let's leave it at that," said Didier.

Camille looked at Didier sideways, since he was never one to shut down any conversation, and especially since he was one to hold us captive with his stories. Her response to Zara made me think of my newfound friendship with Margaux. I understood what she meant, but I didn't agree that one size fits all, since some of us do carry excess wear on our bodies and forcing that newly crocheted shirt to fit would be a struggle. In any case, Margaux would be at the party for Junior the next day. I was certain Camille's eyes would roll to the back of her head when she realised we worked together.

"So, Junior has no idea about tomorrow?" asked Camille.

"He knows we're having some cake. But he has no idea we've ordered food and his favourite tarte flambée. A few people who he hasn't seen in a while will be here," I said.

"I'm so glad he's giving up on this nightclub work and starting the social work program at the university," said my mother.

She had every right to be proud of him. His entire life had derailed after the accident that killed Magalie and her brother, Clément. He had been empty for so long, and finally he was finding himself again, becoming full again, finding love, one that I thought would, despite Camille's concerns, last.

At lunch the following day, Camille offered my mother and grandmother a seat, and then she served them. The meal was rich, Alsatian, and gourmet. My grandmother could do nothing but praise her cooking.

"It's just a little lunch," Camille said.

But it was much more than a little lunch. It was a sharing, an honouring, an investing of herself to those around her. Camille's delicate manner in asking my mother and grandmother to sit and serving them first was more purposeful than any plating or arrangement of food on a dish. It reminded me of all the love surrounding us, keeping us, moving us, of all the efforts that are made for us. It was akin to being on a river, of the river, the river itself deep within us.

That evening, as we were waiting for Anouk and Junior to show up, guests started arriving. When Margaux arrived, I felt a rush within myself, like a schoolboy whose crush had just waved hello. There was something about Margaux worthy of a rush. It could have been the way she spoke, so professorial, never an "um" or a pause, so confident, articulate, charming. Or maybe it was the way she looked, her frame peaking in all the right places, projecting lust. I introduced her to everyone.

"You come to my shop often," Zara said to Margaux. "I thought I recognised you, but I just couldn't place your face."

"I should have said something, but after the first couple of times not acknowledging that we'd met before, I felt embarrassed to then say something," Margaux answered.

I could tell that Zara was put off by Margaux's answer. Knowing Zara, I could feel her mind spinning. When it came to openness, there was a formula of candour and pleasantness that she expected. I knew she was saying, *You come to my shop, knowing you work closely with my husband, yet you don't say a word about it?*

"Surprise!" we all cheered when Junior and Anouk finally arrived at the surprise that was not really a surprise.

They walked in happy, holding hands, full of grins. If they had any thought of keeping their romance private, it was no more. I liked Anouk. She was becoming more deeply imbedded in my family. She was a business partner and best friend to my wife, and now a lover to my brother.

At some point in the night, I caught a glimpse of Camille and Margaux in conversation.

"You're worried she's asking about you?" asked Junior.

"I'd be worried if she wasn't," I answered.

I would not have normally cared, but that rush in my gut made me feel differently. I was finally admitting to myself my attraction to Margaux.

"Look, man, just don't get caught up in no bullshit," he said to me. "Some women don't give a shit."

I heard my brother. That was nothing that the two of us hadn't said or heard before. The same could be said of men. But I knew Margaux better than anybody else did that night, and I knew she just needed a new start. When she and I got to talking later, she admitted feeling seen, like a bouquet of lilies, their white petals arching out of a glass vase.

"Your family is either warm or incredibly curious," she said.

"They are so nosy," I answered with a chuckle. "They want to know everything."

"Your wife is beautiful. Her hair is always wrapped up at her shop, with that beautiful array of colourful green, red, and orange cloths," she said.

"In madras."

"Yes, madras. To see her hair out like that really shows off her face. Other women must be jealous."

When she said that, I was thinking of the conversation I was surely going to have with Zara later, how she would in turn tell me how beautiful Margaux was and how Margaux must make other women jealous, and finally end on her impression of Margaux, that she didn't like her.

When the party was over and all who needed to go home left and the household had gone to bed, with only Zara and me awake, I sat on the couch, expecting her to sit next to me.

"Did you know Margaux frequented my shop?" she asked.

"No."

She eyeballed me, as if expecting me to try a different answer, and then left, proceeding to Eliza's room, closing the door behind her. I would have preferred a conversation, for her silence was metal rain.

The following day, after Zara's parents left for Metz, my grandmother sat across from me at the table. I sensed a sermon coming from the depths of her ire.

"Who is Margaux?" she asked. "And I want the Gwada version, not the Strasbourgeois."

"She works for me."

"Works what, your penis?"

I sighed.

"Boy, is something wrong with you, bringing that woman under your roof, while your wife is across the room?"

"We work together, Nana. We're friends from work."

"What do you think Camille is saying right now?" she asked.

"You can't stand Camille, so what do you care what she's saying?"

"What I feel about her is irrelevant, but we're both women. We're from women. We've birthed women. We understand the struggle of a woman in this man-eat-son-of-a-bitch-dog world. Zara is her child—her daughter. I understand that. I feel that. For that, I care," she said.

My attempt at explaining my relationship with Margaux fell into silence. I might as well have been screaming in the wooded Vosges.

"Margaux is a young, attractive divorcée. That's how it starts . . . just friends. Be honest with yourself, boy. Don't tell me that when you look at her, all you see is a friend from work. Louis Braille could see how you looked at her last night. That's the crap your father would pull."

"I'm nothing like him."

"Your little girlfriend didn't know that, looking like a hyena on the savannah who hasn't eaten for days. Have more respect for your wife. Stop taking her for granted."

"I don't take her for granted. She's my wife."

My grandmother paused and looked at me stupefied, then turned to my mother, who'd sat, silently listening the whole time.

"Widelene, you hear this nonsense? The gall of this boy to say this to me! Do you hear this damn foolishness?"

Then she turned back to face me.

"That's the problem with you West Indian men. You treat your women like pillion passengers on the back of your motorcycle. What does that even mean, she's your wife? So what?"

Jesula Fredeline Bien-Aimé. The only person I knew who could take words, mould them into balls of fire, throw them, and watch them burn. I felt the heat, but I had enough sense to know my place, like on the streets of Strasbourg when the police came by for no reason, asking mundane questions, and all I could do was comply, bend, not be agitated or raise my voice—just be quiet and not react, all so that I could go home.

Chapter 17

There was an underwater current between Zara and me, and it was rising to the surface, readying to crash against a nearby cliff. My attraction to Margaux was just that—an attraction. Other men have done far worse, but here I was being held to a higher standard. There had been no malice in my invitation to Margaux. I didn't have an ulterior motive. Still, I had to endure other people's feelings about Margaux and me, spurring a physiological reaction of a burning rash, like hot oil thrown on my back, moving up the nape of my neck to the crown of my head, all the way down the bridge of my nose, the drumming incessant, like the marching of a thousand threading needles.

The following evening, as I sat at the kitchen table, I watched Zara enter, wash her hands over the sink, dry them by the stove, move to and from the refrigerator, open the microwave, close it, sit down. The banality of her movements reminded me of the little things we do every day that are just as important as the life-changing decisions we make. There was reassurance in the everyday. It was the everyday that sustained us. Thinking those words, it did make me wonder if it was the life-changing decisions that actually moved us. She stopped her movement and faced me.

"Are you attracted to her?"

"No."

We said nothing else with words, but as the proverbial high-noon clock struck twelve, we stared each other in the eye as if staring down the loaded barrel of our guns. The silence of that moment betrayed us both. She didn't believe me, and she knew that I knew. If men were honeybees, Margaux was that honey, her thighs made of honeycombs, dripping honey gold. I was attracted to her. Who wouldn't be, with the frame of an Amazon, her shaved head, brown skin looking like a shade of gold? Parts of me wanted to claim her like one claims destiny or a territory. In a sea of calypso, reggae, and bouyon, Zara was the zouk I loved so dearly. Her Blackness was a staple. It aroused me, sang to me, connected with me. She was the mixed light-skinned girl, whose Franco-German mother and Franco-Guianese father accepted my offer of love for their daughter, offering me peace and security. But Margaux was gwo ka, the beating tribal drum, the ancestors, the African spirit moving through the dancer. She was a Blackness moving like attention while craving none, making her all that more desirable.

"No?" Zara asked again.

"No."

"I won't beg anything of you. They say it's normal for couples in committed relationships to be attracted to other people, to fantasise even," she said.

"I'm sure *they* say a lot of things. I don't know what you want *me* to say," I said.

"Don't humiliate me. It was humiliation enough watching my mother watch you stargazing at that woman."

"Since when are you jealous of any woman I interact with?" I asked.

She stopped and looked at me, ready to spit fire, but instead opted to walk away.

When the summer ended, Eliza started kindergarten. We would soon get used to a quick glance from her, a reassurance perhaps that we were still there, as she lined up with the rest of her classmates before entering the school. She had waited with such impatience to move up to the big school that it now felt so natural, like she had been there the whole time. Her life was in such contrast to Mehdi's, Tatiana's son with my father. He was now thirteen, and the writing was on the wall for him as far as where he would most likely end up in life, in jail or dead.

My grandmother was the only one who kept tabs on him and reported back to me. At some point my father and Tatiana split, and my grandmother, being who she is, provided for Mehdi and Tatiana's older son, David. I helped out where I could out of obligation. Although Junior knew about it, it was not something we talked about frequently, for he couldn't care less for our little brother, not to mention his hatred for Tatiana. And by extension of his hate for Tatiana, he hated the boy. But the boy was innocent in all this.

"Mehdi. That name is supposed to mean 'guiding light.' What light is he guiding?" Junior would say.

But my grandmother knew the backstory. His mother named him because his birth was the light she needed at a bad time in her life, in spite of him being a married man's outside child. My mother never said anything about my grandmother and me helping Tatiana. We never brought it up around my mom. We never spoke of him in her presence. And the day Zara made the mistake of calling Mehdi my half brother, my grandmother swiftly corrected her.

"You mean 'brother.' We don't have half brothers."

It was she who reported that he was too young to be involved with those he was running around with. But there was nothing she could do but counsel Tatiana as best she could.

"You need to reach out to that child," she said to me. "Talk to him, spend some time with him. He needs to know that you care."

"What about Junior?"

"Junior is a grown man. You all are doing wrong by this child."

My grandmother was right. Mehdi was just a child, and he needed to be treated like one. He was not our responsibility, but we were responsible for him just the same. Junior did not think so and felt the complete opposite. There would be no movement there, so I did not even try.

As Christmas drew near, I invited the translation team leaders to dinner. I wanted to know them better. It was part of what I'd wanted since my interactions with Margaux. I invited Zara to dine with us. Initially, she welcomed the idea, but on the day she backed out, as she just did not feel up to it. So there we were, six of us, a mix of language and culture at the heart of Strasbourg, eating, relating stories, the wine flowing among us and on our palates. As the evening petered, Margaux remained the last one at the table with me. We ordered another glass as she moved seats to be closer to where I was sitting.

"I thought Zara was coming?"

She asked the question, her eyes glimmering, lips full. I understood her question to be more of an assertion, like *I'm glad Zara's not here*. I must have paused too long in that answer, and she asked another.

"Did I say that in Russian? Maybe I shouldn't drink that last one."

"No, I just thought you said something else."

"What?"

I shook my head.

"Just my male brain playing games on me."

"Humour me. What's going on in that male brain?"

I shook my head again. I felt her energy. It was red, and loud, and full and sexual. I was getting lost within it. She aroused me.

"Do you love your wife, Salomon?" she asked.

"Very much."

"So why are we still here? Everybody else is gone."

Her questions were direct, and I wasn't sure how to answer them.

"Do you want something from me . . . Mr. Salomon Destin?"

"I'm not sure."

She downed her glass of wine as if it were a shot of whiskey and asked that I walk out with her and help her get a taxi. When we got outside, we walked a bit, just talking. She put her arm in mine and her closeness was warm, her scent percolating my desire, making me imagine her naked body, the endlessness of her brown skin. We started to cross one of the bridges over the canal leading to Cathedral Square and she stopped me, pushing me against the railing.

"The first time you kiss me, I want to reopen my eyes and see more than painted walls inside a room."

We kissed. Slowly at first and then with all the vigour inside me. I wanted this woman. She brought out in me this primal desire, this liberation from the confinement of what I was supposed to be and how I was supposed to behave. We finally stopped long enough to catch our breath again.

"I have to go home," I said.

She didn't plead for me to not go or stay longer. She was very nonchalant in her response. "At least stay until I get a taxi."

When she finally left, a figure approached me, arms open wide like we do when we are in disbelief of something. It was Junior. "Salomon, what the fuck?"

My throat tightened. It had not at all been my plan to kiss Margaux. But there was Junior, a witness to my infidelity.

The following day, he came to the house to drop off a book he had promised to Eliza. The whole time, he barely acknowledged me. When he finally left, I followed him outside and sat in the front passenger seat of his car.

"Salomon, I can't deal with this right now. You need to get out of my car."

"I'm not seeing Margaux."

"Yeah, just her tonsils."

"Listen to me. I can explain. It happened that once. It was a work thing. It wasn't planned."

"You're trying to tell me that since my birthday, you and her haven't been hooking up, that last night was the first time? I look stupid to you?"

"Junior . . ."

"This is Zara, man, Zara—Eliza's mother. She's not some woman that we don't care about. How are you going to do that to her? How do you expect me to show my face here tomorrow, sit at her dinner table, and act like I don't know anything, knowing that you're banging Margaux?"

Junior was consumed with a fire that I could not extinguish. He had no time for what I had to say.

"You're just like him," he said.

"I am not like Dad." That accusation pierced me, because if anyone knew how much unlike my father I was, it was Junior.

"Fuck you, Salomon. Get the fuck out of my car."

"It was a mistake. If you would let me speak, damn."

At this point Junior got out of the car and made his way to where I was sitting. He opened the door and pulled me out, and I scraped my knees as I fell to the ground.

"What the fuck, Junior?" I said as I got back up, shoving him in the chest.

I caught his fist over my right brow. I didn't even see it coming. I stumbled backwards, falling on the hard pavement.

"You wouldn't be like him if you kept your dick out of people who weren't your wife," he said.

I was still a bit unsteady from being punched in the face and was not quite sure I'd actually heard him say what I thought he'd said about Margaux and me. He peeled away, leaving me on the ground as neighbours looked on. I looked over my shoulder to find Zara standing there, before she turned away to head back inside with all the pain of the world on her face, like she had been running behind a runaway train, her lungs full of smoke, tired, hurt, disappointed, bereaved.

I made my way back inside, my knees still wanting to buckle under me, and sat on the couch, my head beginning to pound.

"Eliza and I will stay at Anouk's," said Zara.

"No. I . . ."

"You don't get to speak. You don't get to say one goddamn word to me."

Chapter 18

They say the worst kind of fool is a fool who doesn't know he's a fool. I say the worst kind of fool is the fool who knows he's a fool and can't help but be one. I knew as soon as Margaux and I were alone at the dinner table that we should have gone our separate ways. But being a fool, I ordered more wine. All things considered, the night could have been worse. Of all the ways I secretly yearned for her, in the end, I denied them to myself. A kiss should have meant nothing. I could forget it if she could. But now it meant everything, as Junior had complicated my foolery.

I went to work that Monday, still not having heard from Zara. It wasn't until the end of the day that Margaux, who knew nothing of what had transpired after she and I had parted ways, knocked gently on my door.

"Can I talk to you?" she said, entering my office and closing the door behind her. She sat in the chair across from me.

"About the other night . . . things happen. We're two adults. We don't have to talk about it, ever. We can just bury it and go back to being as we were. I don't want things to be complicated or weird. We can agree we had a moment. I can live with that."

"Zara knows about the other night."

She turned pale. "How? Did you tell her?" she asked.

When I explained that Junior had seen us, and that he had made such a fuss about it in the driveway that Zara heard him, she could do nothing but just look at me and ask repeatedly if I was serious.

"I haven't spoken to her since yesterday evening when she moved in with her friend."

"Did she do that to you?" she asked, referencing my bruised brow.

"No. That's a whole other story. But I have to contain this at home. It cannot spread to the office."

"Of course not. You think I would say anything? I have to work here too."

"Even if you didn't work here."

She looked me dead in the eye. "Are you firing me?"

"I'm sorry, Margaux. This is no easy fix, but we can't work together and Zara and me be OK. I've dissected this in a million ways. It just doesn't work."

"I'm a single mother, Salomon."

"And I don't want to be a single father. We can discuss a reasonable package."

She was shaking her head, sighing, looking over her shoulder making sure the door was closed and that no one could hear us. Her voice was low but firm.

"No. It was a kiss. Zara will get over a kiss. It's bad enough I have to live with the shame of it. You can't fire me over a kiss."

She was flustered, visibly angry. I listened. My silence must have been profound, the way she looked at me.

"Salomon," she said, her eyes somewhere between pleading and disbelieving. "It was a kiss."

But it was so much more than a kiss. It was a fantasy unfulfilled, a fear, a want, a closeness, a carpet full of magic, desire, a weakness men carry in their genes. It was a disaster knocking on my front door. It was a fool's heaven.

Over the next few days, Zara didn't take or return my calls. I contemplated going to Eliza's school at drop-off and pickup times, and even stopping by La Petite Cannelle, but in the end decided to wait. That Friday I stayed home from work, deciding that I would make my way to Anouk's, but Zara finally showed up.

"I'm only here for some clothes and diabetes stuff for Eliza," she said coolly.

"I let Margaux go," I said.

"Lucky her. She just dodged that bullet," she said, not even looking at me.

"It was a kiss. A horrible mistake. I am sorry." I wanted to grab her by the arm, but I knew she would pull away.

"I told you not to humiliate me. Now you expect me to believe that it was just a kiss. Junior doesn't seem to think it was just a kiss."

"Never mind what Junior thinks. I want us to be OK. I miss you and Eliza. I'll do whatever you need."

She looked at me, frustration and pain painted over her face. We were at a place we had promised each other we would never be. But there we were, negotiating a return to normalcy where normalcy may never be the same again.

"Am I not enough? Is what we've created here, our life, our businesses, Eliza, are those not enough?"

"You were right. I was attracted to her. But it wasn't ever to be anything but that. I didn't expect to be in that situation. I never thought it would ever be an issue."

"You're not dumb, Salomon. Don't act like it. You work at the same place. You invite her to our house. Really, it was so inconceivable that you would end up screwing her?"

"I didn't sleep with her. We have never slept together. Ever. And that night was the only time we kissed. I swear it. Zara, I am sorry. I am so embarrassed."

The words came out, but I didn't hear them. I was so deep in my own head, my heart pounding against the walls of my chest, that I had no idea if she heard what I said. I wanted forgiveness, and somehow expected to receive it, but it had become a word, like relief, that until somebody gives it to us and we feel it, we are forever gripped with grief or pain. Zara left shortly after, taking what she had come to get.

Margaux rang that evening.

"Salomon, I understand why you did what you did. You had to look out for you and your family. And I've had to do the same. I had a lawyer review the package you offered."

"Yeah."

"Well, he suggested I be offered more."

"How much more?"

"It doesn't matter. I declined it. We've worked together for years and we've never had an issue. That kiss was as much my fault as it was yours, so I must take some responsibility too. Your offer is generous, and that will give me time to secure another job."

"Thank you," I said.

"Don't thank me. I'm doing this out of care for your family. I don't want yours to end up like mine. Black women have it hard, Salomon. We have it damn hard. And we have to fight everybody to keep ourselves afloat, to make it in this world. Sometimes we even have to fight ourselves."

She was rigid in her tone, as if at any moment she would dole out a punishment. "But I refuse to fight another Black woman. I refuse to fight Zara. And if you're going to replace me, I hope you'll take my recommendation. I'll send you her information."

When she hung up, a wave of relief came over me. By doing for Zara, she had done for me. She had done what I couldn't do for her.

When the phone rang again, it was Eliza sharing the most vivid details of her week. It was the type of conversation that filled me up and the sort of gesture which meant as much as any words of forgiveness. Before she hung up, I could hear Zara telling her to tell me they'd be home the next day. I was barely off the phone with Eliza when Junior's car pulled into the driveway.

He entered, greeting me with a nod of the head. "How's your face?" he asked.

"It's been better."

"Maybe I overreacted."

"It doesn't matter."

"It matters, man. I'm sorry. I'm just tired of bullshit, you know. People saying one thing and meaning the other. I'm so far over being nice for the sake of being nice or to protect other people's feelings. I'm over it."

I nodded to show him that I was listening, but what I wanted to say, the moment wouldn't let me.

"So, for real, you never fucked that bitch?"

"What you saw on that bridge was all there was to it. I never slept with her. Zara confiding in you now?"

"Anouk tells me everything. You fucked up, Number One."

"We can't always win."

"How do you guys go back to being OK, though?" he asked.

That question was one which ran through my head constantly. As much as I wanted to curse Junior, I knew that he seeing Margaux and me that night saved me.

"There is nothing else for me to do," I said. "I can only be here, as present as I possibly can, be a better husband and a father."

"I don't know if I would ever get over it," said Junior. "I mean, it would always be there. People forgive, but they don't forget. And you know how it is—when they get mad or feel down, that's the first place they go, to that place, you know, that you all thought was done and dealt with. And you, my brother, just served that girl some blood pudding, and that shit is runny as fuck."

I nodded, made a sign he should follow me into the living room, and sat down.

"I hear you, man, but sometimes that's the burden we bear, kinda like reparations. We have to give in and understand that our fuckups are not the responsibility of others. If they hate us for it, it's their right."

"You're making me think of Colette Bishara. She rightfully hates me."

"You still think about her?" I asked.

"It's the way she doesn't see me. If she could chop me into pieces and feed me to Mr. Moïse's pigs, she would."

"You can't let that tragedy control your life, though. You're moving on, but you have the brakes on, like you're afraid to be happy. The past is done. You can't undo it. Colette Bishara was Colette Bishara before her children died. She didn't like us back then when they were alive, she doesn't like us now. I feel for her, especially now that her husband is dead too, but really, Colette would hate you regardless."

He listened and seemed to absorb my words.

"What if you and me did something together? Like go somewhere we've never been before?" I asked.

"Like where?"

"Anywhere, doesn't matter."

There was something between us that needed to be aired. There was a stuffiness, a certain rank smell, something just not right, like an airless bedroom in the middle of a Strasbourg winter. The storm between Zara and me was just another complicated layer of my relationship with my brother. We were anything but cut from the same cloth. Though I ignored it, it still bothered me to hear him refer to me as "Number One." I was not. I just fell in line and did what I was supposed to do. There was nothing about me that made me Number One. But that's what he saw. That's what he had always seen.

"Remember that old TV we used to have?" he asked. "The one we had to connect to a car battery?"

"And recharge the battery every night. Yeah, I haven't thought of that in a long time."

"Long time is right. Crazy thing is, it hasn't been that long ago. Now we're hiring and firing people, buying trips, sending money back home to raise other people's bastard children."

He was smiling while saying this, and I wasn't sure where he was going with it.

"I liked the uncomplicated ways of our poverty," he said.

"But we were never poor."

"Like hell, we were never poor."

"I wasn't fucking poor."

"Oh, Salomon could never have been poor. You carry too much shame to admit that," he said.

He was bothered by my reaction to his words. It was a subtle reaction—just the expression on my face. It seemed to sting him. I felt that maybe he regretted saying them as soon as they fell out of his mouth. And that is exactly what they did, fall out like dense metal teeth out of gooey gums. They were ugly and foul, and utterly unnecessary.

"We didn't have a lot, but we never went hungry. We always had clothes on our backs, went to school and played. We were happy. They taught us to live with dignity."

"They, who?" he asked. "Only my mother showed me how to live with any dignity. We. Were. Poor. We were no different than those people living by the mangroves in their aluminium shanties. Wake up, Number One!"

"Man, I'm getting tired of you calling me that shit."

I wanted to reach across the room and flog him, knocking the smug smile off his face.

"I guess I hit a nerve, huh? How you want to be right with your wife, but you don't want to accept the reality of who you are? Be right with yourself . . . brother."

But I was right with myself. I was as right as I was ever going to be. Junior was what my grandmother used to refer to as a tap dancer—people who never quite understood their role in life, making a pile of noise and saying nothing. And Junior was tapping on my last damn nerve.

"You don't know me, Junior. You really don't know me."

"I know I'm not the one you should be planning any trips with."

That comment forced me to take in a deep breath.

"Forget the trip. I'm trying to meet you where you are and do right by you. You suffered a tragedy. But damn, man, I'm here trying my best to help you pick yourself up—been trying for years. Not just for you but for me too, for all of us," I said.

I didn't know how else to tell him how much I loved him, how much he was the light in all our eyes, how much we needed him.

"I don't need you to change me," he said.

"I'm not asking you to change. I don't want you to change. You and me, we don't have anything to change for anybody. But we're here, man. We're here. We've made it this far."

He put his hands up in protest and then crossed them several times, denying my words. "Listen, man, all I want is to go back to that battery-operated TV. I don't care about what we had or didn't have. Maybe you don't want any change, but I want to change the past," he said.

"Junior, brother, I love you. Black men suffer enough. There is no need to change the past or ourselves. We need to stick together and rise from all this shit. We have to wash off the stink. Only we can make our lives better. But brother, take the help that you're given."

It seemed like once again, two people were talking, but neither spoke each other's language.

"You've never had to deal with shit, Salomon. The closest you've ever come to having any shit on you was when you shoved your tongue down that Russian girl's throat. What the hell you know about shit? Man, I killed two people."

"That was an accident."

"Salomon, listen to me!" he said, insistent that I never hear him. "I killed Colette Bishara's two children. It was my fault. The car in front of us was slow as fuck that night. They told me to just stay there and follow it until we got to Boucan and we would go sleep at their cousin's house and not have to drive all the way back to the city. But I didn't listen. I overtook that car. They would be here right now had I just listened and done what I was told."

Junior had built walls everywhere, the greatest perhaps being himself. But that evening, a truth came over him. The tap dancer wasn't just making noise. It was a well-choreographed display of movement and sound, from hard to soft, quick to slow, shallow to deep. His audience listened. I listened. Tears filled his eyes, but they would not fall. They were there, like a bookmark between pages, with words highlighted, a reminder to me that I didn't have diabetes, that I didn't kill two people in a car accident, that I didn't spend two years in a detention centre, that I was never on probation, that my father never made me feel like he hated me, that all my brother wanted was a damn alkaline battery–operated television.

Chapter 19

Pointe-à-Pitre, January 2010

"Gadé guèl a salop-là!" my mother said under her breath as she hunched over my father's casket. There were no tears, but she had the handkerchief in her hand, in case they came over her maybe, or not. She held the side of the casket, her hand trembling. My grandmother came over and told my mother that he, my father, didn't deserve my mother's sadness. Whatever pain my mother felt, it was one that none of us could understand. They had had good days and had seen their own share of tragedy. They had us, Junior and me. My brother didn't come to the funeral. Surely, it would have hurt him to see my mother hurting so much for a man who caused her so much pain.

"Just cry, Mom," I said.

"I can't cry for that dry bag of bones."

But trying so hard not to cry usurped her calm being. I walked outside with her, where she no longer kept it in, leaning on me for support. She was just regaining her composure when Mehdi rode up on his bike. It was his father's funeral, but he wasn't attending. He had just come by to take a look at the scene, according to him. He was several blocks away from home. He looked haggardly; the stench of a male goat that hadn't been castrated enveloped him. His feet were so dry, they looked white; his toenails were yellow and hadn't been cut for weeks. He looked homeless.

"Is it true that Junior didn't come?" he asked.

My mother just side-eyed him.

"It's true," I said.

"Mehdi, when last you bathed?" asked my mother. She was impatient.

"Why didn't he come?" he asked me, ignoring my mother.

My mother cocked her head. First, she looked at me and then at him. The audacity of this boy to ignore her.

"Junior is a grown man. It's up to him if he wants to come or not," answered my mother. "And I'm sure he bathed this morning."

"Fritzner doesn't deserve a funeral. My mother is in there, and I don't understand why," he said. "No one should cry for that man."

He spun his bike around and rode off.

"How could Tatiana allow the boy to just let himself go like that? If that's how he is at fifteen, how does she think he'll be in three more years? These women don't know the first thing about raising a boy right," she said.

After the funeral we came home, and my mother went to lie down. It was just me and my grandmother in the living room. She sat in her rocking chair.

"For what it's worth, I'm sorry you had to come home and bury your father. It's not the last time you'll be coming down to bury family. That's the curse of getting older. We die and you must bury us."

"Junior feels nothing for the man at all," I said.

"Why are you acting so surprised? You can't blame a tree for not bearing when all you do is beat on that tree."

She arranged the blanket over her legs. The acceptance that what he once wanted from Fritzner was never going to come.

"That was one sorry funeral, though, if you ask me," she said. "When I die, I want to hear Mr. Jean's gwo ka from beyond the grave. My heart will finally stop beating late in the night when you all go to bed."

"You're never gonna die, Nana. Soukounian can't die."

We both laughed.

"Well, I've been called worse than a witch. Some of these young boys coming around here think I'm one, or that is what they choose to call me, those little bastards. They think I can't hear them and that I'm half blind. But I see them making *kabouyas* with grass reeds and throwing it over their shoulders when they see me coming. I told one of them one day that after two hundred years, I've mastered not being impacted by a *kabouya*. The little shit screamed and ran to his house."

We laughed again.

"God will punish me," she said.

"I'm sure God is laughing with you. This new generation is something else. Talking about new generation, Mehdi rode up on me and Mom when we were outside the funeral home. He looked homeless."

"*Looked* homeless? That boy sleeps where he can. I don't even think he goes to school anymore. Fritzner played fast and loose with all these women, didn't care too much what damage he left in his wake."

"You think there are more children?"

She looked at me, sighed, and closed her eyes as she leaned back into her rocking chair.

"Boy, the man is dead and buried. Please don't look to raise the dead."

I sat there for a while and as her breathing settled to a gentle snore, I went under the veranda, where I climbed into the hammock. I closed my eyes and let the breeze rock me to sleep. I missed the beautiful nature of my Gwada, this land that nurtured me, received me into this world, and watched me become a man. I thought of Arthur Rimbaud's poem, about the dead soldier in the vale, half smiling, head bare, two red holes in his right side, while nature gently rocked him, as if he were an infant. I thought of that image, of me lying there peacefully, and wondered if Mehdi had ever been rocked like that, had he ever felt tenderness, if he could ever find peace. And then I dreamt I was with him, on the windiest of days, and I helped him make a kite. We broke two blades off a coconut tree leaf and cleaned the spines until there were no blades left. Then out of brown paper, we made the sail. We then measured one spine to length and used it as the kite's spine. The other we used as a crossbar, bending lightly, using tape to hold both spines in place. We added an enormous tail and four small holes for the thread. The whole time, Mehdi was watching me, not saying a word. I looked at him and at this time he was crying. I tried consoling him, but he kept on pushing my hand away. He wiped his face on his short sleeve, and it was then I realised his tears were blood. But for some reason, that didn't perturb me. I was more concerned with him crying. When he stopped, he took the spool of thread and I ran down the street in the opposite direction, kite in hand, holding it up against the wind.

"When I throw it in the air, just give it a tug, like when you have a fish on your line. The higher it goes, just release more string and keep on tugging. Release and tug!"

The kite sailed into the air. His tears turning to laughter and joy. And then I could not see the kite anymore, it was so high into the clouds. I turned to Mehdi to ask him if he could see it, but he was nowhere to be seen. I started calling his name and woke myself, nearly falling off the hammock onto the tiled veranda floor.

"You one of those people who can't sleep in the day?" my grandmother asked, she too having awoken from her slumber. "Your grandfather was like that. He would have some wicked dreams too. Scared me more than they scared him."

"Had the strangest dream about Mehdi."

"That little boy shaking you like that? And I'm the soukounian?"

Mehdi did shake me. There was a part of his story that bothered me. Even though I sent money to his mother, a job that should have been my father's, it clearly wasn't enough. No amount of money could help Mehdi. That's not what he needed. He needed my brother, my Uncle Yves, my grandfather, me—men who could show him love. He was craving it, and my father offered him nothing.

"Where is Tatiana's family?" I asked.

"They're country people. Sainte-Rose, all the way up the Sofaïa."

I wanted to offer this boy something more than just the island heat of this country. He didn't have to be one of the lost ones of the archipelago. He had potential to be great. He didn't have his father's build, but he had his mother's gentle face, this innocence that was wanting to be flayed at every question, every mark, every time he walked out of his front door. His hair was loose upon his back, and if we didn't know his father was a Black man, he could pass for full East Indian. The danger with him was the anger he harboured within himself, and I wondered if it was all because of our father.

"Boy, I see you're trying to raise the dead. When they come for you, don't say I didn't warn you," my grandmother said.

"He's fifteen, Nana. He deserves better than this."

Now that my father was buried, I would be leaving for Strasbourg in two days. I carried this strange guilt about Mehdi and couldn't help picturing him dirty and ashy and smelling like a drunk. I sought him out the day before I left and asked him if I could buy him some clothes. He was keen on the idea, but I said he would have to shower because no store would allow him inside in his state. We drove to the Destreland Mall in Baie-Mahault, just outside the city centre, not too far from our neighbourhood.

"You've been here before?" I asked him. He shook his head. "You've been to the other parts of the island?"

"Not really. I used to go to Sainte-Rose with my mom, but I don't anymore."

He said this as if it were not by choice, as if something was keeping him from wilfully going.

"Why don't you go anymore?" I asked.

"Ask them."

We left the mall with two bags of clothing and shoes. I could tell he was excited about his purchase, although he didn't want to show it.

"Where can I get a real good *bokit*?" I asked him.

"You have to go back to the city, by the open market. This old woman sells them. She's always dressed in madras—can't miss her."

It had been years since I'd had the fried sandwich filled with shredded codfish and pepper sauce. It had been years since I'd had so much of what made Guadeloupe home for me. I barely dipped in the ocean. I barely bathed in the cold river as it ran down the mountains. I couldn't tell you when last I ate barbequed meat with hot vinaigrette sauce burning my lips and tongue, or the last time I ate a sweet, succulent guava, a grafted mango, or flying fish smoked outside on metal wire. I left this country at eighteen, and though I returned often enough, I was becoming a stranger to it. I wish I had more time here, alone, without Zara and Eliza, so I could take the time and reconnect with it—maybe even drive to Sainte-Rose and take a drive up the Sofaïa to the mountain and lie on the beach after in Deshaies. These are all things I've done in my youth. And here is this broken boy, a prisoner to his own neighbourhood—a victim of inaccessibility.

We ate and drank a couple of orange sodas, then headed back to his mother's place.

"Why does Junior hate me?" Mehdi asked.

"Junior doesn't hate you. He's just a bit hard."

"No. Ma' Jesula was talking to me in her yard one day and on one of his visits, he chased me away like I was some dirty chicken crapping all over his veranda."

"What did he say?"

"To get my dirty Indian ass out of his mother's yard. I don't go there anymore."

He spoke like a man who had been to war. His lack of affect and blank stare sent a chill through me at times, as if my gut was telling me to be mindful of Mehdi. But he was my brother. I may not have known him that well, but he was my blood nonetheless. He was a child.

"If I send you a ticket to Strasbourg this July, would you come?" I asked.

He shrugged.

"Mehdi, you have to see more of the world than just Pointe-à-Pitre. You're stuck here in your little corner of this city, and that's not what life is about."

His head was down, looking blankly into his lap. "All right, I'll come," he said after a short while.

"But between now and June, you have to go to school."

He looked at me with that same chilling cold and shook his head as if to say, *Of course, there's a catch.* "Fine," he said.

When July came, Mehdi stepped into the waiting area with his luggage. Zara and Eliza were also there to meet him. He seemed uncomfortable with these strangers smiling at him and touching him. Eliza was especially excited to learn that she had another uncle.

"I won't see Junior, right?" he asked me shortly before bed.

"I don't know, but no one is going to shoo you away."

As I lay in bed with Zara, she too affirmed what I had thought about Mehdi, that there was something off with him, and anyone who actually saw him could tell that he wasn't altogether right.

"I'm not surprised, given what I understand of his life. I didn't realise Fritzner was such a horrible human being," she said.

"He wasn't always, or he hid it well, but the alcohol sure brought it out."

"That boy needs some therapy."

"Yeah, but not everyone who has no facial affect is a potential cold-blooded killer. We brought him here to know him a little better and show him there is love for him. Let's start there," I said.

After a few days of visiting the Strasbourg area, we visited Metz for a few days and stayed at Zara's parents' place.

"I thought this place was farmland when I first heard about it," I said. "I wasn't sure I wanted to marry a farm girl."

We laughed. Mehdi laughed too. He was becoming more comfortable with the family, playing more with Eliza, even being alone with Zara and not seeming anxious.

We arrived to more smiles and touches, and he seemed better with this. Didier and Camille were warm as usual.

"Where's Grandpa?" asked Zara.

"At the park playing pétanque with the other grandpas. He'll be back soon," answered Camille.

As the afternoon went on, Didier was over the moon in having a listener to whom he could tell the history of Metz. He had told me so many stories that I jumbled them up in my brain. I could never keep them straight. And then I heard him tell Mehdi the one that I do remember about the imperial wing of the train station that was used only seven times. He delighted in talking about the imperial train and especially about the Roland statue, the one that was decapitated three times after Metz changed hands between the French and the Germans, as each country wanted it to look like them. Mehdi listened. I don't know if he actually listened or just bided his time in captivity.

When Zara's grandfather Aubain walked in, he immediately set about telling Mehdi that he didn't have to listen to Didier's stories. Didier smiled at this mammoth of a man. He was tall and large, his skin dark, like mine.

"So you're the good-looking brother. That's why they kept you in hiding," said Aubain to Mehdi, who let out a small grin. "He told you about the Roland warrior yet, the one that's had four heads because the Germans just wouldn't go away?"

"Yes."

"You'd think after the second time, the Germans would just say 'to hell with this!' and go away. Persistent little buggers, weren't they?"

After supper, Aubain, Mehdi, Eliza, and I sat in the living room. Eliza was sitting on me when Aubain started talking.

"You know, when you're mixed, people either like you because you look exotic, or you have nice hair, or pretty eyes or whatever. Or they hate you because you're different. Don't let people's perception of you define you. I know at your age that's hard to hear, but even if you don't accept it, you should still hear it. You have one life to live, son. I wish somebody had told me this when I was younger. I spent half my life chasing other people's dreams and what they thought I should be. I left Guiana to chase the lightest skin in a skirt I could find."

I had already discussed Mehdi with Aubain and had asked him to share his experience. Although this conversation seemed to come out of nowhere, it had been planned well before our trip to Metz.

"You see me, black as night. I never thought I was enough," Aubain said, after a brief silence. "And even though I felt inadequate within myself, I still looked down at the native Guianese, like I was better than them. These people were in Guiana long before Europe colonised the place. I was just a descendent of slaves brought to their island to work for nothing, but still, I looked down on them. I thought I was better. So the first chance I got to get out, I did. And when I got here, I read Aimé Césaire expressing what I was feeling, only that he realised that France was not the solution."

He paused momentarily, like a preacher searching for the right words to deliver the ultimate point of his sermon.

"The solution," he said, looking Mehdi square in the eye, "is to realise our self-worth."

Mehdi was attentive. Even Eliza seemed entranced with her great-grandfather's words.

"France is definitely not the solution," he continued. "But it is an option. And for options, you need an education."

Aubain got up and went to his bedroom. He returned and handed a book to Mehdi, who held it carefully, looking at the title.

"Ever heard of Joseph Zobel?" Aubain asked him.

Mehdi shook his head.

"Well, he wrote a hell of a good book there. *La Rue Cases-Nègres* is my favourite. It's a classic in my view, right up there with works by Hugo, Balzac, and George Sand. There is a film adaptation too, and the author makes a cameo appearance as a priest. You will like it. Keep the book, and next time you visit you can give it back to me."

Mehdi was thankful and appreciative of Aubain's kindness. It was my hope that some part of that reached him and that when he returned to Guadeloupe, he could stay as much as possible on the straight path. I knew it would be hard without support. But at the very least, the conversation was had.

When we returned to Strasbourg, I found him to be contemplative while uncharacteristically anxious. I wished that Junior could see Mehdi and treat him like the child he was and not like the consummation of Junior's problems.

"Are you all right?" I asked him.

"What if I can't be perfect? Will you guys stop liking me?"

In spite of the stoicism in his face, his eyes were pleading. The child who was wanting love, compassion, and acceptance stepped out and asked the world to keep him.

"No one is asking you to be perfect. We can't ask of you what we are not. We all make mistakes, like you have and will continue to do. The key is that you have people to support you through those mistakes, like I have, and Junior, Zara, Jesula. All of us needed support at some point."

"But what if it's bad?"

"I don't know what bad is. Stealing is bad. Murder is bad. Getting a girl pregnant at fifteen is bad. Don't worry so much about what you could do bad but more what you can do right. But I will say this: You're turning seventeen soon, and before you know it, you'll be an adult. The older we get, the heavier our mistakes. And unlike some folks we don't have the luxury of certain mistakes. You get what I'm saying?"

He nodded. I wondered if I should have been more explicit and said that we don't have the luxury of being white, and that a Black person committing the same crime as a white person would be prosecuted more harshly. I wanted to tell him that the road he was on was one of destruction, that he had one foot inside a jail cell and the other inside a grave. Instead, for fear of being his father, I talked about the luxuries we couldn't afford. I just wanted to be his brother.

The following day, we walked to La Petite Cannelle to show Mehdi where Zara worked and to introduce him to Anouk. When we opened the door, Junior was there sharing a laugh with Anouk and a customer. The atmosphere changed instantaneously, in concert with Junior's demeanour. Right about then, Anouk acknowledged us and called out to Zara, who was in the back room, she herself not sure what to do. Junior turned around and left.

"Go ahead and play house!" he said to me under his breath as he was leaving.

I followed him out.

"Junior! This is fucking stupid. What the hell? He's innocent in all this. Give the boy a break!"

"I can't see that fucking kid. Don't ask me to. I just fucking can't." He walked faster in front of me, hardly turning around to respond.

"Give him a chance, man. How do you think he feels right now?"

"It's not even about him. It's all he represents. He's that love child that nearly killed Mom. You don't think of that?"

I grabbed his shoulder as he unlocked his car, to which he turned around. "Fine, but you don't have to treat him like shit," I said.

"I don't want to treat him like anything. I don't want to know him. I don't want to see him. I don't want to give a shit about him. So go play house all you want, just leave me out of it."

And with that, I watched him climb in and drive off, wondering what I could say to get through to him. I turned to head back into the shop, and there was Mehdi staring at me, his expression as blank as the Roland warrior from Metz.

Chapter 20

Strasbourg, November 2010

It had been four months since Mehdi left and returned to Guadeloupe. Whenever I spoke to him on the phone, he seemed at a better place within himself. My grandmother and Tatiana confirmed that he was going to school again and even sleeping under his mother's roof once more. Tatiana was happy with how things were turning out, but the tone of her voice over the phone suggested some apprehension.

"It's not him. It's the people around him," she said. "It's the corner store where the men sit all night and drink rum. It's the boys sitting on the curb doing nothing all day, just smoking marijuana. And most of those boys are his friends. And he joins them. I can't tell him not to because now he's back in school and sleeping here again. I don't see it lasting."

That was my fear too, that after a while he would go back to the life he knew, one that had little consequence, one that was easy and didn't need to be worked at.

For our part in Strasbourg, life went on as usual. There was little change except that I was missing Margaux's support in the office.

"The new Russian team leader is a great translator but not a good leader. Her team keeps coming to me. I have my own shit to do. I can't keep her," I said to Zara one night as we lay down to sleep.

"Don't you dare fire her," said Zara. "Don't be that man. Bad enough you managed to get rid of a single mother already."

"We're doing this again?" I said, aggrieved, sure my disappointment was painted on my face.

"Why don't you talk to her and teach her? Did no one internal want the job?" she asked, her question more of an accusation.

"A few applied, but I didn't want them. They're all too friendly with one another already. They're too tight. I have a business to run."

She looked over at me, pausing, as if to pool her thoughts before raining them down on me. "With everything else you're so open and hopeful and flowery, as if the universe gave you galaxies for eyes, but for your business, it's black and white—so cutthroat."

"Failure is not an option, you know that," I replied.

"Yes, but these are people."

"People who are my employees."

"Don't be an ass. I hate when you get that way."

"What way?"

"Stubborn and stupid," she said, then rolled over and ignored everything else I said.

The following day at work, I received a text message from her.

> -Sorry about last night. I know that Margaux was not a business decision. Just sometimes I think about that situation, and it makes me angry. But you hired this new girl because she was impressive and Black. Do right by our people.

This was one of the many reasons I knew Zara was the right one for me. Even when I didn't feel I needed support, I had it. Even when I didn't want it, I had it. Even when I could do without it, I had it. Even this woman—this new girl—who had no idea I was on the verge of firing her, had support that she never even knew about. It bothered me to think of Mehdi, on the cusp of crashing again, not seeing that his friend group was not supportive, not understanding that his mother wanted only the best for him.

-And maybe stop referring to her as the 'new girl'. What is her name?
-Katia
-Well then, have a frank conversation with Katia.

When Katia and I met in my office, I told her my concerns. Initially, she acknowledged what I was saying as truth. But then, when I mentioned giving her support, she shook her head.

"You don't agree about me supporting you?" I asked.

"It's not that. My team, they talk. They feel one of them should have been internally promoted instead of me getting the position as an outside person. They won't say it, but they think I got the job because I'm Black, like the last person . . . Margaux? It's hard to motivate people who don't respect you."

"I hired you because I felt you were the best fit. And Margaux actually recommended you. You didn't know her, but she'd had eyes on you for a long time."

"Yes, but I'm starting off with a roadblock."

"Katia, people like you are hard to find. There aren't too many Black translators who speak Russian. And yes, as much as possible, my management team will be Black. You have to get comfortable with that. Too many white people get positions they don't deserve. They get them because they're white. They get them over brilliant, competent Black people, like you. At best, they're mediocre, but they're still celebrated. I guarantee you've been passed over for promotions, and the one who got promoted still used your expertise after the fact. They still used you to do their job—a job that should have been yours from the start."

"It's very frustrating."

"I know. I've been there. That's why I opened my own business. You are part of my management team. If they don't like it, they can work somewhere else. I don't micromanage. You don't need my permission to hire or fire. This is Strasbourg. These racist motherfuckers are replaceable. That is your team, and you are their team leader."

She seemed surprised by my words, her eyes the last dots to finally connect to what I had just said.

"OK," she replied.

"This is not a roadblock. This is the sort of systemic crap that makes us question and doubt ourselves, or feel like we can't do what we're supposed to do, or we have to be careful about hurting white people's feelings, or stop taking crap, or just saying no. This is not a roadblock. This is an opportunity to build something, to be a part of something, to stand up for something. You see what I'm saying?"

"I do. Thanks. I needed to hear that."

"I know I'm probably preaching, and pardon my language, but seriously, fuck them!"

When she left my office, my hands were trembling. I was furious with her team, but I felt good about connecting in that way with her. She wasn't Margaux, and our connection was certainly different, but I knew what she had to offer, and I was so grateful for listening to Zara in how I dealt with Katia. Had I gone guns blazing, trying to save what was mine, I would have killed everyone—captive, guerrilla, missionary.

We spent that Christmas in Metz. Junior and Anouk went to Guadeloupe to spend it with my mother and grandmother. Their plan was to go to Dominica after Boxing Day for a tour of the island. On Boxing Day, however, I received a call from my grandmother, exasperated.

"They want to go to Dominica tomorrow, but I don't know. They got in some hell of an argument earlier," she said.

"About what?"

"That little Bata-Indian boy," she said, using a term used to describe Indians mixed with Blacks.

"Mehdi?"

"Apparently some of the boys were teasing Mehdi about his murderer uncle when Junior walked by and Mehdi lashed out at them, trying to fight them all. Well, they beat him pretty bad, and Junior just walked by like he didn't care."

"Poor Mehdi."

"Yeah. I guess he shoved Junior, telling him he was fighting for him. And Junior just ignored him. Anouk said she couldn't believe a grown man could act like that towards a seventeen-year-old. She said she felt so bad for the boy that she put her arm around him and asked him if he was OK. She helped him get ice to put on his face."

"So they argued about that?"

"Well, she told him she's not going anywhere until he goes to see the boy."

"Oh my God. He's not doing that."

"That's one thing you can't do, give Junior an ultimatum. So he left. It's been a few hours now. She's been trying to call and text, but he's not answering. I told her to take back that ultimatum and work on him slowly. I hope he comes around soon, before he lives to regret it."

I tried calling Junior myself but didn't get an answer. When I called Mehdi, to check on him, Tatiana said that he hadn't been home. I told her what I'd heard from my grandmother, and she sighed.

"He's most likely at Mr. Moïse's place. I'll walk down there with David and see if I find him."

"OK. Just call back and let me know. Don't worry about the time."

She called back about an hour later, saying that he was asleep at Mr. Moïse's and that his face was swollen, and he was badly bruised. She said she would return in the morning to check on him.

"His own friends," said my grandmother, after I called her the next day to tell her where Mehdi was. "Those aren't friends. Yes, he lashed out, but to beat him up like that? And they're not all his age. Some are grown men in their twenties. Well, I hope that makes him see them for who they are. I have to go to Mr. Moïse about some pig snout soon. I'll see how he is."

As for Anouk and Junior, they caught the ferry across the Dominica Channel to Dominica. No one knew what the outcome of their argument was. When they returned to Strasbourg in the new year, they spoke of the wonderful time they had on that mountainous island with its rivers for every day of the year. And then Anouk showed us her engagement ring.

"Junior proposed after we'd hiked a few hours to the boiling lake."

We offered our congratulations, and I wondered how come neither my mother nor grandmother had said anything.

"They were sworn to secrecy," Anouk replied. "Though we feared Jesula may crack before we got here."

I was surprised too and maybe a bit disappointed that she hadn't told me and made me swear to act surprised.

"We're getting matching tattoos too of Dominica's native name, and the date of our engagement. Wai'tukubuli: December 30, 2010," said Anouk.

We ate lunch and spent the day talking about Dominica, Guadeloupe, and Guiana. We were laughing and content on our peaceful family Sunday. No one brought up Mehdi, but in the back of my mind, he sat there like a heavy load, percolating like words full of thunder and lightning, waiting for a chance to rain.

By March, Anouk and Junior were in the midst of their wedding planning scheduled for the end of August of that same year. They agreed Strasbourg would be the most central location, as they both had family travelling from overseas. Some of Anouk's family flew in from Côte d'Ivoire. Others who had dispersed to various areas of France made it to the wedding by simply booking a TGV. The actual wedding would take place just outside of Strasbourg, in an old quaint church which opened to a magnificent view of extensive farmland. Junior and I drove there one day, to measure for a tent in case of rain. We were looking at where to put it and the position of the sun in the late afternoon. It took the greater part of the afternoon, and before we headed back to the city, we stopped at a café to eat.

"So you're just gonna avoid asking me about what happened with Mehdi?" he asked.

"I know what happened. No need beating a dead horse."

He pursed his lips and nodded.

"I won't push this kid on you if you don't want to know him. Just don't treat him like shit. I'm more interested in the ultimatum you were given."

"Damn. Nana's still fucking nosy like that?" he said, shaking his head. "I heard what you said outside the shop last summer. I reflected on it. I had decided that if I ever see him again, I would be decent towards him. Nothing more. But then those assholes called me a murderer. And that stung me, man. I went right back to that courtroom, when that *béké* judge said I was troubled and had a history with the law and was not surprised to see me again, like the rest of them. If it was up to him, I'd face a tougher punishment. All he saw was this Black motherfucking menace. I was guilty before he even heard my case."

"So you heard that, and you just said, 'Fuck it'?"

"Pretty much. If Anouk wasn't with me, I would have probably broken the guy's face who called me a murderer. I wasn't even thinking of Mehdi. And when he came up and shoved me . . . oof . . . I almost smashed him, but he had that dead look in his eyes, that cold-hearted monster look, and I froze. My feet may have been moving, but inside it was like he shot me with a twelve gauge."

"I've seen that look. Makes you wary of him. I just remind myself that he's a kid."

"He's not that young. But anyway, when I calmed down and explained all that to Anouk, she understood. And thank God for Dominica. We needed that."

The late August wedding was all that a late August wedding in France could be. The sky, the air, perfume mixed with the scent of heat, polished shoes, and a zest of sweat and hair. Brown skin glowing under cocoa butter, strangers and friends greeting and mingling, the bride and groom repeating their original vows, words inspiring us to look within, at ourselves and our own relationships, planting seeds in desert plains, where we can grow like baobabs. Anouk's dress was trimmed with a bright madras cloth, the colour of the Caribbean, paying homage to her husband's heritage. When the minister declared them husband and wife, and they kissed, a long, dragged-out kiss, my grandmother shouted, "Leave some for later!"

The lights set up around the perimeter of the wedding venue came on as the sun started to disappear. Zouk, Haitian, and African music were pumping through the speakers. A few French and English songs made the cut here and there, and guests were dancing as much as the alcohol was flowing.

"You've been part of my life longer than you've known Junior," I said to Anouk as we shared a dance.

"I'm grandfather-claused in if shit goes south. Remember that," she said.

"We always keep the better half in this family. You're good."

We laughed. She was right, though. She'd been grandfather-claused in from the moment I met her. She was Zara's best friend and business partner and now my sister-in-law. She was family before she even knew she was family, before we even knew she was family. That's what family was—people whom we trusted and loved, and for whom we would lay down our life.

When the festivities came to an end and guests were all but gone, Junior and I walked a bit past the last lamppost delineating the perimeter.

"I have to thank you for this day," he said. "Not too long ago, I never saw myself alive today, let alone marrying anybody."

"I didn't do anything special, brother."

"You believed in me, and no matter what, you kept on pushing. I'm a social worker now working in a system that nearly fucked me up. Where would I be if not for you and Zara?"

"That's the least I could have done, brother. It was a huge learning curve, and had I known what I know now, I would have done things differently. But we're here. That's what matters."

One of the last two taxis pulled in.

"Go be with your wife. Take that taxi home. We'll take the next one," I said to him.

Junior and I watched as the cleanup crew stacked chairs away, Eliza sitting on a chair, oblivious to what was happening around her.

"I'm surprised she didn't go with Mom and Nana," Junior said.

"Too much excitement. There was no way she was leaving."

"She'll be a great big cousin."

I agreed.

"In about seven and a half months from now," he said.

"Fuck off! You're serious?"

He was all smiles, his grin as wide as the farmland in the distance.

"Congratulations!" I said, my heart full of joy as we hugged.

The following day, the house was in a constant state of jubilation as Junior and Anouk broke the news of their pregnancy to my mom and grandmother.

There was much change happening in our family. Junior and Anouk were leaving for Dominica the next day for their honeymoon, the island on which they were engaged, one which they wished to discover from the city centre of Roseau to the rising green mountains of Calibishie. In a few more days, my mom and grandmother would return to Guadeloupe, and it would be Zara, Eliza, and me again, in the quiet of Strasbourg suburbia.

Chapter 21

October 2011

Junior called me from the hospital in the middle of the night. Anouk had experienced cramps and bleeding, so they rushed to the hospital. A few moments later after a closer examination, they were told that they had lost the baby.

"They're prepping her for surgery right now. She still has to deliver the foetus," he said.

All I could say was "sorry" on repeat. Zara was looking at me, her hand over her mouth, her eyes swelling with tears. We were all devastated. The worst was that they would have to tell people about their loss, and I didn't know how anyone could ever be ready for that.

"They're young. They'll try again," my mother said, when I broke the news to her and my grandmother over the phone. "My poor baby. I don't know whether to feel sad or sorry."

She was right. They were young and they could try again, like the millions of people who suffer miscarriages and try again. But in the meantime, their hearts were breaking for a child whom they had named, whom they had pictured in their minds how she would love and speak and act. They knew she'd learn to speak Kréyòl from a young age and that she would know where she came from. She was to be a fighter, a social justice warrior, a woman of her own means. She was to bring joy and comfort to the people around her. So many things they had imagined of their baby girl, and all I could say was I was sorry. All the world could say was that they were young and could try again.

It took Zara and me some time explaining to Eliza what happened to her Uncle Junior and Auntie Anouk's baby. We had been trying as gently as we could to put it in a way that would not traumatise a seven-year-old, only for Anouk and Junior to come for dinner and be very blunt about it.

"Sometimes it's just the body's way of telling us that the baby wasn't healthy enough for the outside world," said Anouk. "It hurts our hearts, but it gives us a chance to get stronger and prepare for another one."

"So you'll have another baby?" asked Eliza.

"Well, you can't be the only little person around here."

The two laughed and embraced. After dinner, Junior and I went outside by the driveway.

"It's funny how everything is so connected," he said. "Our lives are so linked. Not just because we're family but the things that happen to us, our jobs, education."

As he spoke, I listened, not quite sure what point he was trying to make.

"Mehdi. Since doing this social work program, I see him in much of what I do. And now, actually working as a social worker, there are so many Mehdis out there. And they don't need much. Sometimes, food, safety, someone to keep them centred."

"Ah, Mehdi. He stopped taking my calls. He stopped going to school again, hardly sleeps at his mom's place."

"I fucked up there," Junior said.

He was ashamed of how he had treated Mehdi all these years. He was ashamed that after his last visit to Guadeloupe he hadn't gone to see Mehdi to explain the misunderstanding of ignoring him. But now, he had clarity. It was a clarity he did not need manifesting the way it did, full of shame, regret, and guilt. Junior was still reeling from our father's betrayal of our mother. He was still trying to cope with the hatred our father had for him, and to be asked to love Mehdi, knowing who Mehdi was, was a big ask. Finally, he was there, but I didn't want him to be there like this. Mehdi wasn't his burden to bear.

"Whatever happened to Mehdi happened to Mehdi a long time ago. Don't beat yourself up about how you didn't treat him right."

"Man, I'm gonna have kids one day. And if ever they fuck up and stray, I don't want anybody looking at them like they're scum," he said.

"We're never going to control what people say and feel about our children. As long as we teach our kids that after they fuck up and know better, they do better. We can't control the world, especially this white world. We have to manoeuvre the best we can."

"I'm ashamed of myself, man. I owe that kid an apology."

That Christmas, Zara, Eliza, Anouk, Junior, and I all went to Guadeloupe. My grandmother had not been doing well and kept talking about how it would be her last Christmas. No one believed that to be the case, but we all felt sufficiently guilty that we flew down. Much to our chagrin, she had to be rushed to the hospital soon after we got there. She'd suffered from low blood pressure and stayed a few more nights at the hospital. She was released before Christmas Day, but the house had not been the same without her. Even having her back, we were more tepid than usual in our celebrations. My mother was worried. That was the first time she'd had to call an ambulance for my grandmother and feared it would not be the last. She remembered calling an ambulance for our Uncle Yves, and more recently, how Colette Bishara called an ambulance for her husband, who would never make it back home. My mother was anxious.

On a few evenings, we saw Colette Bishara entering Mr. Jean's front door and then the drumming would start, and then another, more faint and more unsure, would follow. Some evenings Mr. Jean's front yard would be filled with people. Some drummers were sitting on the barrel of their drums, while others sat in chairs, their drums between their legs. They would drum all night, singing in Kréyòl, akin to old spirituals. There were occasions a woman or two would dance, holding on to their long skirts, waving them as if to fan their thighs. On nights like these, Colette Bishara did not drum. She looked on like the rest of us and, when it was over, slowly walked back up to her house, this place which had become near derelict, boarded up. That was the first sign of change for me, when the holier than thou participated in rituals straight from the shores of the African continent, when the uppity Black woman joined the rest of us, doing what we do—what we have always done, what she forbid her own children from doing.

"Is drumming all you're showing Colette Bishara over there?" my grandmother asked Mr. Jean as he joined us under the veranda for Sunday lunch.

Mr. Jean smiled. "She promised me a bread pudding from her sister weeks ago. I'm still waiting."

"If only that was the question you were asked," my grandmother said.

"Old woman, leave the man alone. It's Sunday. Don't bring no nasty talk here today. You see Eliza sitting right there?" scolded my mother.

"You think people don't have sex on Sundays? If memory serves me right, I'm pretty sure you were conceived on a Sunday."

"Mom!"

"The day after the Sabbath!" Mr. Jean said, laughing. Then seeing my mother unimpressed, he said, "Don't upset the cook, Jesula. I'm getting used to these Sunday lunch invitations."

"Uh-huh. Are you now?" said my mother.

"This is lovely. It's good to have family around," he said. "We're just playing, Widelene. This is really good. Thank you."

My grandmother rolled her eyes. Mr. Jean, though, was being sincere. He had two grown daughters who he no longer talked to. It had been years.

"Colette has been good for me. We eat, we drum, we talk. I wish she drank too, but she won't touch that stuff. But it's good to talk about the past, no matter how painful it is. It's like a personal redemption," he said. "We're so conditioned to think of forgiveness as a two-way street. No. I can live happily where I am because I learned to forgive myself, even when others wouldn't forgive me. Colette taught me to allow myself to be vulnerable."

"Colette who?" asked my grandmother.

"Mom, stop."

"Colette-Colette? Bishara?"

"Yes, Mom. Stop it."

"She's lying."

The rest of us couldn't help but laugh. Our laughter was like the scattered wind which found us under the veranda that Sunday. It came and went, finding us in the shade in spite of the heat.

"And so, I did," Mr. Jean continued. "I opened up and put everything on the table. I felt what it meant to be naked in public. I felt the shame of being watched. But afterwards, it felt so good."

"When last you saw those girls?" asked my grandmother.

"Too long. Close to twenty years. I wasn't to be the example of love. Their mother said my love was the worst kind of love. She was right."

"It takes strength to do what she did, and even more strength to respect it," said Anouk. "It was the same thing with Maxim. There was a time when I worshipped the ground he walked on. He could do nothing wrong."

My grandmother looked at my mother, her eyes questioning who Maxim was.

"Her last husband," my mother said quietly, to which my grandmother nodded.

"He could not want for anything. I was in love. I had found somebody who made me happy, somebody who seemed to love me for me. But I wasn't ready for that kind of love. I didn't love myself enough to love somebody else. I was so young."

"He was so old," said Zara.

Zara and Anouk laughed.

"So, what I thought as love was just me clinging to attention—his attention. I sort of lost myself, and in doing so I gave him permission to do as he wanted. I gave him permission to mistreat me."

"And boy, did he ever!" said Zara.

"That's the burden placed on us," said my mother. "It doesn't matter how good of a woman we are; some man will always find a way to crush us. As if this Black skin isn't crushing enough."

"Some men don't know what they have until it is too late," said Mr. Jean.

"That's what happens when you put them in the field to cut the cane, and then promote them to oversee the rum in the distillery, then sell that same rum at the corner store, put a table and chairs outside that corner store for them all to sit, spend their money, and drink, just to give the *béké* back what little he paid them in the first place. Ain't nothing changed," said my mother.

"You're right," said Mr. Jean. "That man might as well be back in the field busting his back under the hot sun."

"And when he comes home, he just takes all his frustration out on his woman. As long as *békés* run this island, women will never have a chance," my mother said.

There were four generations of Black women under the veranda that Sunday. Ultimately, their conversation on Black femininity ended on the hopes they had for Eliza, that she may never feel like she needs a man, that she may never fear a man, that she may never give herself to a man unrequitedly. And it wasn't just the women who thought so. As Mr. Jean spoke, his regret was instruction for Junior and me. It was a map littered with fault, but his faults were stars burning bright, like the beacon of a lighthouse over miles of open water in the darkness.

My grandmother had gone for a nap in the late afternoon, when we talked about her care. Her body may have been falling apart, but her mind was still sharp. We watched as Colette Bishara entered Mr. Jean's house.

"There she goes again," said Junior.

Somehow, my mother sensed there was more behind his observation.

"Don't worry yourself with Colette. No one knows the scriptures better than the devil," she said. "We're basically sacrificing our pride for the greater good of our spirit. And Colette is so proud. I don't see her sacrificing her pride for any greater good. Even if it meant doing so would give her spirit peace. But who knows?"

"Yeah, who knows? Maybe she's just barely hanging on."

"Well, you know better, so you do better," said my mother.

She had become teary. Her internalisation of Junior's pain and her mother's ill health were beginning to manifest outwardly. As strong as she was, she could not hide her pain. She sat at the kitchen table, Zara and Anouk standing on either side of her, rubbing her back and shoulders.

"I'm grateful that you children all came down. When the old woman talks her nonsense about dying, we dismiss her, but she needs you all here today."

"We're happy to be here with you and Jesula, Widelene," said Anouk.

"I knew I should have had one more child, one that would have stayed close to home. Soon you'll all be gone back to your big city lives, and it will just be me and the old woman. And when she goes, it will just be me."

"Mom," said Junior.

"Mom what? Who will call the ambulance for me?"

Just then there was a knock at the door. It was Colette Bishara.

"Speak of the devil," said my mother, as surprised as the rest of us.

"Good evening, everybody," said Colette Bishara. "I see we have a full house. How is Jesula?" she asked.

"She's fine," my mother answered. "She's resting. Not quite herself."

"I heard the news and I felt horrible, especially this time of year, and you children down," said Colette Bishara.

She stood in the doorway and took a deep breath. My mother, recognising that she wasn't just passing by, invited her in. She sat down across from my mother, a package wrapped in a kitchen towel in her hand, and the rest of us just watched. Junior looked on. He rested against the kitchen sink and folded his arms, his expression, mildly stoic. My mother caught my eye for barely a second yet betrayed all the uncertainty of her emotions towards Colette Bishara's visit.

Colette Bishara placed the package on the table. "I was glad to hear that you children came home this Christmas. Too bad your visit is dampened by your grandmother's illness. I'm sure she's still glad to see you."

She looked at Junior and me.

"I hear the kids nowadays calling me soukounian when I walk by. I don't blame them. Lonely old woman living in that boarded-up house by herself. I remember you two calling me that. I pretended not to hear you. I never believed in that stuff anyway—the voodoo and the drumming and dancing all hours of the night. But then my Magalie and my Clément died, and I was in grief for years. I couldn't even grieve for François when he died, a man who dedicated his life to God and helping people through their most difficult times. I couldn't find enough peace to grieve him too. I was still grieving the loss of my children."

My mother leaned forward, her forearms on the table, and tilted her head slightly, in full attention to what would come out of Colette Bishara's mouth, who at this point reached across the table and grabbed my mother's hands. My mother looked uncertain.

"I was still hating your boy, Widelene. I was still hating your child for killing mine."

Colette Bishara started crying. My mother's expression of uncertainty turned to one of sorrow, as this woman sat at our kitchen table and laid her demons bare.

"No one can fault you for grieving," said my mother.

"Thank God for Jean," she said as she looked towards Mr. Jean's house. "He invited me in even though I cut my eyes at him. He was patient and talked to me about what drumming does for him. When he beats that drum and sings his Kréyòl, I forget what pain I carry. And then we talked about forgiveness. Me, a Christian woman, a pastor's wife, a mother, unwilling to forgive another mother's child."

I looked over at Junior, who had not moved from the kitchen sink. He looked back at me and grimaced slightly, uncomfortably.

"We see you all the time going to Mr. Jean's. Hearing the gwo ka and the singing, the old woman and I did think you had turned a new leaf," said my mother.

"It's more than a leaf, Widelene. My whole life has changed. I am asking your family for forgiveness. I'm sorry for all of it." Then turning to Junior, she said, "I forgive you."

She fell short of adding "for killing my children." But it seemed at the tip of her tongue.

"Thank you, Mrs. Bishara," said Junior. "That means a lot to me."

Then, in the same strange breath, she turned to face my mother again.

"Well, I figure I might as well kill two birds with one stone," she said, unwrapping the kitchen towel from the package on the table. "It's my sister's bread pudding. I just gave one to Jean. I know your family loves it. It's my peace offering and well wishes to Jesula."

We could see the moistness of the dark surface, the raisins bursting out of the top, and that hint of Gwada rum, sparsely whipping at our nostrils.

"I hope you enjoy it. It's time for the old soukounian to get back to her hole," she said.

She left and we were quiet. Junior was still by the sink, shaken and emotional, as Anouk comforted him. My mother went over and embraced him too. And he started crying like a child.

"Come, come, my baby," she said softly. "It's OK. It's OK. You're all right."

She held him, as they both stood there in the kitchen, rocking as if they were slow dancing in place, their feet stuck to the laminated floor. We all looked on, Zara and Anouk in each other's arms, Eliza in mine. Junior's tears were nearly twenty years of grief born of the fatal accident which took Magalie's and Clément's lives. It was the sorrow of not being able to give Colette Bishara back her children. It was a pain, so rooted to his core, time could do nothing to separate it from him or alleviate the chokehold it had on him. He needed to hear Colette Bishara forgive him. He finally could forgive himself. When he and my mother finally let go, we heard my grandmother's door open.

"The old woman's up," my mother said. "Just in time. Somebody, get a knife. Let's cut this bread pudding."

"How was your sleep, Jesula?" asked Zara.

"I think I had a nightmare about Colette Bishara being in this house."

My mother sucked her teeth.

"Nightmare my foot. You heard her. You weren't sleeping."

"Still a nightmare."

"Mom!"

We laughed because clearly, she was back to her old self, and we couldn't ask for anything more. My mother cut the bread pudding into slices.

"We're not eating that bread pudding," said my grandmother.

"Why not?" my mother asked.

"Just because you cut an alligator's mouth doesn't mean it's not still a long-mouth alligator."

"She was sincere, Mom," said my mother.

"Maybe. Time will tell," she said, as she picked up the sliced bread pudding and threw it out the window. "If that damn soukounian thinks she's getting anything over me, she's sadly mistaken."

"Woman, what the devil is wrong with you?" asked my mother. "You couldn't stay in bed another ten minutes?"

The rest of us stood there silently, palates whet at the smell of that bread pudding now outside for any stray dog to eat. Zara and Anouk were somewhat shocked, but Junior and I smiled. That was Jesula, our grandmother.

The afternoon of Christmas Day, Junior and I walked to Tatiana's with small gifts for her, David, and Mehdi. We were not surprised that Mehdi was not with them. Tatiana was even more worried than before, that he would get himself in more trouble. She found him one day at the kitchen table wiping down a handgun.

"He didn't seem bothered in the least," she said. "It was like I wasn't even there."

We walked down to Mr. Moïse's place and there Mehdi was, roasting a goat on an open fire with the old man.

"That's a lot of goat for two people," I said.

"People will come down later," Mr. Moïse answered. "They always do. I'll have to bring some for your mom and grandmother. How she doing?"

"Much better. But she would definitely like that."

Mehdi didn't acknowledge us. Mr. Moïse went in to fetch some rum and shot glasses and poured four shots.

"Mehdi, leave that goat alone and come over here!" he said.

Mehdi sauntered over.

"Merry Christmas!" we said to him.

Mehdi nodded his head, though he did not really acknowledge us. We drank, and immediately after, Mr. Moïse poured us all another. He had already smelled like rum when we got there. We had another and refused more. He was about to pour another for Mehdi when I suggested he go easy on the boy. Mehdi poured himself one and downed it too, and went back to tending to the goat.

"Sometimes that boy can be so simple," Mr. Moïse said to us. "He's been by that fire for hours. It won't cook any faster. But no sense telling him that."

I left Junior and Mr. Moïse and walked over to Mehdi. "Man, I miss our phone conversations. How you been?"

"I'm all right."

"We got this for you," I said, and handed him the gift.

He opened it and seemed initially delighted. It was an iPod with a gift card for downloading songs.

"Thanks."

"Junior wants to talk to you."

"I'm here."

I waved to Junior to come over and rejoined Mr. Moïse under his veranda. I couldn't hear what they were saying, but Junior was doing most of the talking.

"That boy is troubled, you know," said Mr. Moïse. "I let him come here and drink his rum and smoke his weed because it will keep him out of trouble. When he's here, there is no trouble. Some other boys had started coming down here, but I ran them off my property. But trouble likes him and follows him. It's only a matter of time before something bad happens."

"I know. He was doing well for a little while."

And Mehdi had been doing well for a while. Mr. Moïse's words were a disappointing truth. I started to feel guilty for not doing more for my young brother, a guilt which was slapped into shamedom by Mr. Moïse's follow-up words.

"If he had grown up when you boys were growing up, he would have flourished. But these days, there are too many vices that steer them off the straight and narrow."

"I don't fucking need you or your shit!" Mehdi shouted at Junior. He threw the iPod to the ground and pushed the roast-spitting goat to the ground with his foot. "Fuck the both of you!" he said, and marched up the hill.

"To hell with you, you little shit. After all I do for you, that's how you repay me? *Sakré Voyou!*" said Mr. Moïse.

We helped Mr. Moïse get the goat back on the spit fire and left, leaving Mehdi's gift with him, knowing that he would come back, even if it meant with his tail between his legs.

Later that night, my mother answered the phone. "Oh dear. In Baie-Mahault. Anybody hurt? My dear God help us. OK. I'm sorry to hear that."

She looked at us, her face full of despair.

"That was Tatiana. Mehdi was arrested in Baie-Mahault for shooting at somebody. That poor boy."

Chapter 22

Pointe-à-Pitre, February 2012

My grandmother was admitted to the hospital again. Every time I saw her, she was more fragile than before, aging faster seemingly than the frequency of my visits. It pained me to see how age had also come for her so slowly, so debilitatingly, but life was ephemerous that way, breathing grace and beauty into the same flower it let wilt away. The doctor made it clear to us that another Christmas would be a miracle, and that as much of a fighter as my grandmother was, her spirit had no fight left.

"You're flying down too often," said my mother. "You need to save your money."

This from the same person who was lost for words at the thought that her mother may be admitted for a while, this same mother who wanted out of the hospital for fear she may die there.

"I don't want to die in no bloody hospital. I want to die in my house. I want to hear Jean playing his gwo ka when the good Lord come for me," my grandmother said from her hospital bed.

There was anxiety in her voice, like my childhood fear of open water rising past my chest, my toes gripping the sand, my body swaying at the mercy of the waves.

"God, I hope she'll be able to hear them," my mother said. "She needs a distraction from all these memories of her past. Must be the flashback of the life we see before we go."

"When we were children, Yves and I watched a man fall out of a coconut tree, smashing his head on the dirt ground in front of our grandmother's house," my grandmother said. "Yves told me not to go to him, but I went anyway. The man had this gurgling sound in his throat, like he was trying to breathe but for the blood in his airway. His eyes were wide open, staring at me. For months, all I saw was those eyes. Now I see them all the time."

She was weak and started speaking inaudibly, after which she closed her eyes and fell asleep.

"That's not all she's seeing," said my mother. "She thought I was her mother the other day."

When we brought her home, she became much calmer again, the anxiety of dying anywhere but her home all but gone. She continued sharing her stories. These were stories she never shared with anyone. And they were pouring out of her like a river after a hurricane, full, strong, and wide. It was then she told us about Fabiola, her grandmother.

"When Yves and I were children, we spent most of our time at our grandmother's. She wasn't the kindest woman, although she was kinder to me than to Yves. Poor Yves. He suffered under Fabiola. She didn't like him. Yves was always a little soft, you know, but he was a good boy. Any trouble, he would take up for me. If one of us had to get licks, he would take mine and say nothing. Fabiola liked to punish him, and any chance she got to beat him, she took it. And it wasn't just her rod; her words were just as vicious. She called him 'Yvette' and 'little woman.' She cursed at him whenever she felt the need to. We all knew Yves wasn't like the rest of the boys. I, for one, knew he didn't like girls the same way other boys did, because one time I saw him and another boy from the city under the bush. When they saw me, the other boy took off running like somebody was trying to shoot him with a slingshot. I swore to Yves and to heaven and hell that I would never tell a soul what I saw."

My mother and I listened without interrupting. Uncle Yves's life was the secret that was not really a secret. I didn't know for sure, but I knew. It was like knowing what orange marmalade would taste like before spreading it on your bread, parts of the rind both bitter and sweet resting on your palate. It was like that with Uncle Yves. We never asked or talked about it. We knew.

"Yves and I stayed in that bush for the longest time. When we finally returned home, Fabiola was waiting. We weren't even close to the house, and she was already shouting *makomè* at him, strap in hand. The other boy was there. He had gone and told Fabiola that Yves tried to touch him. Yves and I denied it. I even said I was there and nothing like that happened, but it didn't matter. Poor Yves got strapped that day for doing nothing but expressing feelings for someone else. I don't know how he managed to live under Fabiola, but I know he hated her—we both did."

"Things got better for him, though, Mom. He was OK," said my mother, trying to reassure my grandmother about Uncle Yves.

"Better? My gentle, precious, loving brother never had the chance to live a full life. For all the things he knew about the world, he never experienced the joy of a true companion. His life was something he kept to himself. Before he died, he told me he still remembered that day, and hung on to that memory. Not Fabiola or that other boy, but of him and me under the bush, realising who we were to one another and that no matter what, we were family. After all that time, all those years, the hurricanes, earthquakes, floods, mudslides, all the political corruption and assassinations, all the things that would make somebody go 'To hell with this! I'm living my life,' he still lived under that bush. It was never better for him. Not for him."

My grandmother's face sank in sadness, knowing that her brother had done much more than not live his true life, knowing how much he had sacrificed for her happiness, how much he had sacrificed his later years for their mother, veiling a resistance from the Tonton Macoute.

"I will see him again and when I do, he will be happy. His dreadlocks would have grown back, and his face full again. I know he will be waiting for me after the last drum beats. I'll see them all, him, Mirlande, Robensen."

She looked at us from her rocking chair.

"We will all go at some point. And we will all face our past. When Robensen was dying, all he talked about was Mirlande. I can't speak for Fritzner, but there's no way that man didn't have regrets about you all. I regret not being strong enough for my brother and not pushing him to be who he really was. I helped him hide for too long under that bush. And maybe I was too harsh with Colette. Who knows, maybe she did change? I don't think anybody should spend their last days worrying about what should have been. That's not right. At my age, dying should be at peace."

So many dwell under that bush. Some hide, afraid of being found out. Some lie there, sheltering from the sun and rain under the giant shade of root leaves. For others, it is comfort. It is the resistance found in resting, doing nothing, not working themselves to the bone. As much as my grandmother felt that Uncle Yves never got up from under the bush, she herself never left. She was right there with him. Perhaps why they remained so close.

"These aren't your last days, Mom," said my mother.

"What, you're going to keep them from me?"

My mother rolled her eyes, shaking her head.

The following day I went to the juvenile detention centre to visit Mehdi. I sat at the metal table and chairs fastened to the ground and felt the cold dreariness of the place. It wasn't that different from a secondary school classroom. There was no warmth, just what the visitors brought the inmates. While waiting for Mehdi, I watched several young men be greeted by their families. They weren't much older than Mehdi, but I could see the longing in their faces, the need to be out of that place.

A door opened, through which Mehdi entered. His plaits were undone, and his long black hair fell like a shawl across his back. A guard accompanied him to the visitors' area, holding him by the arm. As they approached, Mehdi shook his body so as to rid himself of the guard's grip.

"Ti-Zindien, foutéw bien!" said the guard.

"My name is Mehdi. And I'm not your fucking Indian."

The guard looked at him hard but chose to swallow whatever words were clamouring at the base of his throat. Mehdi sat down.

"They have no respect in here. These guards are animals, but they treat us like we're the animals," he said.

"You have to keep your head down," I said. "Telling a guard to fuck off won't help your situation."

"I shouldn't even be in here."

"Mehdi, you shot at somebody."

"I missed."

"It's attempted murder. People saw you shooting at him."

"Not if they can't find a gun. And they ain't never finding that."

Between the shooting and his arrest, Mehdi had found time to get rid of the gun. I wanted to ask him why he shot at somebody, why he had a gun, who gave him a gun, but I knew those would only take us to where we could only fall on our faces.

"If I wasn't your brother, you would hate me like the rest of them," he said.

"If I wasn't your brother, I wouldn't leave my dying grandmother to come sit by a jail cell with you. People don't hate you, they're just tired of your bullshit. Your mother is frustrated. What else can she do?"

"I mean Black people. You guys hate us Indians. You hate me cause I'm mixed."

His youth and naivete surfaced through those accusations. He had no idea that East Indians in the Caribbean came as indentured servants, and, as bad as some had it, it was pale in comparison to what the African slaves endured. Whatever he felt of himself, I would still be socially inferior to him. Black folks were always at the bottom of the barrel. But he did not see this. His experiences did not allow it.

"Your entire existence is within a twenty-mile radius. That's the only world you know. I can't say what you feel is not valid, because that's what's been your experience, but the idea that Black people hate you or think less of you? Who owns most bus lines? Tell me, who do you see driving the buses? Besides the *béké*, who owns property here, farming land, cement companies, warehouses, who? Black people don't have anything to hold over you. And to those who think they do, I say to hell with them. Focus on who loves you for you, who thinks about you, misses you, cares for you, wants to be with you. Think of those people and the joy you bring them."

He looked down at his hands. "How's my mom?" he asked.

"Worried sick. Worried they might keep you, that you may lose these years of your life. She blames herself for how your life has turned out. We all do. I know I do."

"You? Why?"

"Because I was having the greatest life in France when you were trying to cope with the insufferable."

"That's why you're here now?"

"We all want to be here. You're one of us. The reason doesn't matter. I'm here, Zara's here, my grandmother, my mother, Junior—we're all here."

"Fuck Junior! He's an asshole."

"He wants to make things better between the two of you."

"He doesn't want to feel guilty anymore, that piece of shit. He tried apologising at Christmas by Mr. Moïse's place, but I told him to keep his apology and fuck off."

I could hear my grandmother telling my mom and me about dealing with our past, not waiting until that moment when we're ready to cross to the other side to have it weigh on us.

"You said Ma' Jesula is dying?" he asked, after a brief pause.

"She's old. Looks like her time is near."

"She didn't use to have much time for me. I would call her 'soukounian' and she would call me '*voyou.*' But then she would visit with Mr. Moïse, and if I was there, she would start talking to me. Things got good between us when she saw Fritzner slap me one day."

"What happened?" I asked.

"Not long before he died, Fritzner came down to Mr. Moïse's place and told me to go home, not like he himself was ever home. He said I needed to change my ways, listen to my mother and go back to school, sleep in my own bed. The usual garbage talk."

"Why did you stop sleeping there?"

"She doesn't stop nagging me. Wants me to go back to school. What's school teaching me?" He shook his head, sucking his teeth. "Nah. That ain't my home. Ain't never been my home."

"Don't call it home, then. Just call it a place to eat and sleep and wash. You're old enough to keep to yourself. Talk to your mother and brother. You all figure out some boundaries. It doesn't have to be difficult. But it's better than being in here, isn't it?" I asked.

"It's hard to live with my mother. It's hard to respect someone who kept on taking Fritzner's shit. It's better if I stay out. People feel sorry for her and shit, but she ain't all that good. And David is just as spineless."

The mention of his mother took him away from the initial conversation about my grandmother and Fritzner. There was a missing piece to this puzzle that he needed to provide, but then he segued back full circle.

"I respect Ma' Jesula. I wish she was my grandmother. I don't respect Tatiana. She let that man beat on me and said nothing."

"I'm sorry."

"He came to the house one day. His girlfriend parked on the side of the street and waited for him. He wanted that stupid engagement ring back. It wasn't the first time he came for it. My mother kept refusing to give it back, not like she even wore it. She didn't give it back just to spite him."

"And what happened?"

"I told him I took it and dropped it in the crowds at the bus depot and that most likely somebody found it and took it."

"Was that true?"

"No. But it didn't matter. He grabbed my collar and slapped me across the face. I thought punches hurt, but when a grown-ass man slaps you in the face with his open palm, you feel it."

"And she did nothing?"

"Not enough, like she always does. She gave him the damn thing in the end. I got slapped for no damn good reason. So I left for good. Mr. Moïse didn't mind me sleeping at his place, so I stayed there. But then that asshole decided to come find me and tell me that I should be sleeping at 'home.' When I told him no, he laid more slaps into me. That's when Jesula stepped in. His girlfriend was in the car watching, engagement ring on her finger. Jesula ate him up and spit him out for his girlfriend to collect. Ma' Jesula saw him do that to me once. In all the times my mother has seen that man hit me, the best she could do was give him back his damn ring. Fuck her."

"You're saying 'fuck her,' yet you're asking how she's doing," I said.

He was an old soul trapped in a boy's body. He felt the weight of the world in all its despair. It was now a matter of survival. How was he to move forward? It would be perhaps the hardest question he would have to answer.

"That motherfucker is lucky he's dead. I want to unbury him and kill him again," he said.

"You don't want to kill anybody, especially not your father."

"Did he beat you guys too?"

"I knew two Fritzners. The one you knew all your life, I only met him when I was a few years younger than you are now," I said. "The alcohol changed him for sure."

"Well, I'm done with people treating me like shit, especially the Black people around here who look at me like I'm some dirty Indian. One of these days I'm just gonna shoot one of them in the face."

Chapter 23

Pointe-à-Pitre, May 2012

Mehdi was released in March on condition he stay at his mother's house and that he return to school. He had no choice in the matter. It was either that or be reincarcerated. I spoke to him over the telephone several times, and his disdain for his mother clearly burned deep inside him, nearly as much as his hatred for Fritzner. He was home, but even that felt like a prison, worse perhaps, than if he had remained in custody. He was almost eighteen, and though now too old to force to attend school or do anything, the other option was less appealing. My only hope was that the fear of reincarceration would be motivation enough for him to attend.

My grandmother was on a steady decline, and we had to face the reality that she would not be with us much longer. We hired a nurse to ease the burden off my mother, but the nurse could not ease my mother's pain of losing her mother or of my mother's loneliness. By May, we were asked to go to Guadeloupe and say our goodbyes. My grandmother's time had come to finally leave this world.

Mr. Jean and his company played their gwo ka in his front yard, the drums, once again, tearing through the night. When some of the men sang, it felt as if they were wailing for their own mother, as if they felt my grandmother leaving us, and they wanted to play for her, or for us, or for both.

"You hear how they're calling for my death?" my grandmother said.

"They're calling for your life," I said. "They're holding on to the night for you."

She paused in reflection of the moment, exhaled, looking nowhere in particular. "I'm ready," she said, her voice like an afternoon breeze, blowing softly. "I'm ready to go home."

She slipped in and out of consciousness. We started pouring into the bedroom to be there in her final moments as she transitioned from this world into the next. Jesula Fredeline Bien-Aimé, a woman whose veins were made of cast iron, who saw more misery than the entire room collectively, lay there, her breath increasingly shallow. The drumming was synced to her breath, and when she took her last, it stopped, and in doing so, passed the matriarchal crown down to my mother, whose tears at this point were all the years of sadness she ever kept.

In the days following my grandmother's passing, we held her wake. People came from all over Guadeloupe and Haiti to pay their respects. Tatiana showed up with David.

"My condolences," she said. "No matter the circumstance of one's death, it is always a tragedy to lose someone dear to us."

"Thank you," said my mother.

"The world needs more Jesulas. She was very good to my boys, especially Mehdi."

Her other son, David, did not say anything.

"Anyway, we should go. I'm sure the last few days have been very long for all of you," she said.

"Where is Mehdi?" asked my mother.

"I don't know, most likely at Mr. Moïse's. I hardly see him anymore. He's on the streets with the rest of them, going up and down all day, doing nothing. He barely comes home."

"He looks at me sideways every time he sees me," my mother said. "I think it's all the prayers I pray for him why he hasn't thrown a brick at my head yet."

"He is angry," said Tatiana, "very angry."

"He is more than just angry," said Junior. "He told me he would make me eat the fire that was meant for Fritzner. His exact words were *'Ou ké manjé dzifé là'* as he made a sign of a gun with his fingers and pointed it at me. I can only imagine the fire to be a bullet."

"You and your father look so much alike. When he sees you, he sees Fritzner. Sometimes, I don't think he can see a difference. I feel like I'm losing him to himself, and these streets, and for good. I'm not ready to bury my child."

"Nobody is ever ready to bury their child," said my mother.

"I know how he feels, like the whole world is against you," said Junior. "I remember not being able to look at you and your children, Tatiana, and not feel like my blood was on fire. I want to make this right with him. I want to include him and let him be an uncle to our baby." He reached for Anouk's hand.

"You're expecting?" asked Tatiana.

"Yes, four months."

"Congratulations."

It rained that night. It was a soft rain, like fingers tapping on the galvanised roof. It was a sound I loved all my life, one I missed when I moved to Strasbourg. It was a relaxing sound, one which helped me fall asleep and which often allowed me to reflect on my day. I wondered if it was the same for Mehdi. Was rain on the galvanised roof soft for him too, or was it hard and agonising, rife with pain and irreversible scars?

The following day, I was walking from the elementary school playground with Eliza when Mehdi passed us slowly on his scooter. He looked back and casually turned around and came back our way. As he approached, I could smell the rank off him, his cigarette hanging for dear life on his tobacco-stained lips. His hair was in thick braids again and was starting to mat like dreadlocks, his eyes bloodshot.

"You remember me?" he asked Eliza.

"Yes."

He rode on, made a small loop, and came back to us again, like a shark in water, sizing up its prey.

"Sorry about Jesula. She was all right."

Before I had a chance to say thank you, he kept on moving, only this time he did not loop and come back.

I spoke to Zara about the encounter later that afternoon.

"Bringing the cow to water is hard enough, let alone making this one drink," she said. "I hate to say this, but Mehdi may just be one of the stories we regret talking about. We can only do so much."

My grandmother's funeral was in three days and although I grieved her, I was also grieving Mehdi. He was the reflection of pain, brokenness, a cage, and he didn't know how to deal with any of it. I went to Tatiana's that night, hoping that Mehdi would be there. I climbed those same three steps and stood under the same veranda where my father and I drank that night, when he confessed the truth about Mirlande, where Tatiana, then carrying Mehdi in her belly, told me I should take my father back with me. To this day, I still wonder if our lives would have been different if I had.

"I don't know where he is. Most likely, he's at Mr. Moïse's place," said Tatiana as she stood in the doorway with David.

"He hates that you all act like some kind of bourgeois people. Before you went to France, you would piss on the side of the road, like the rest of us," said David, looking at me like I had insulted his mother by coming to her front door.

He whispered into his mother's ear and walked out, closing the door behind him. In the past, he rarely spoke or even addressed us, but now he was front and centre. His forwardness was out of character to me. He seemed out of place.

"As far as I'm concerned, my father died in that distillery fire," he said. "Nobody wanted your father except for my mother. She blames him for Mehdi, but you're all responsible. You all are. I wouldn't blame him if he shot the whole lot of you in the face. But then I would lose my brother, whatever I have left of him."

"He's my brother too," I said.

"Your mother didn't birth him. So fuck you!"

I said nothing else and walked away.

Late in the morning, the following day, I walked down to Mr. Moïse's with a cold bottle of guava juice and a baguette sandwich of ham, cheese, and butter. There Mehdi was in a makeshift bed of rank sheets, sweating alcohol from his pores. As I got closer, his eyes opened. He rubbed them, perhaps thinking he was dreaming. When I handed him the food, he was still looking at me as if confused by my presence. He put the food down and walked to the far edge of the veranda, where he proceeded to urinate in the bush.

"Oof," he said. "I got to find myself a shower. You know when you can smell your own nuts that's when you really stink. Lord have mercy on these nuts."

I couldn't help but chuckle at this boy's idiocy. In spite of his nasty, stinking self, he had a sense of humour that reminded me of Junior. He came back for the food and sat at the other edge of the veranda from where I was and started eating.

"Thanks for thinking of a brother, brother," he said. "I don't even eat ham, but fuck me, this is good."

I don't know how he managed to taste anything. He barely chewed it. He must have been famished, because he inhaled the sandwich.

"Why don't you eat ham?"

"Rasta don't eat no pig."

"Since when are you a Rasta?"

"Since when you come down here asking me fucking questions?"

"It's just a question. How long have you been a Rasta?"

He ignored me and bit into his sandwich some more. "How old is Eliza now?"

"Eight."

"She looks happy."

"She is."

He ate some more.

"What if you came to France to live for a while?" I asked.

"And leave all this?" he said, looking around. "So I can see more cathedrals and statues without heads?"

"No. So that you can be around family who care about you and who want you to have a better life. I want you to know your niece better. We all want to know you better. I don't want you at the mercy of the courts down here."

He side-eyed me. I must have said something wrong, as he contorted his face in disgust.

"What courts? Courts said I should be living with my mother. I don't live with my mother. Courts said I should be in school. I'm not in school. Even the courts could give a shit about me, man. I want to go to Dominica and live in the mountains, like a real bushman—nobody to bother me."

"At least come by the house after the funeral. Come see everyone."

On the day of the funeral, the heat itself was searching for a place to hide. *O swè là sé dzifé nou ka manjé.* Those were the words inscribed on my grandmother's casket as it lay in front of us, adorned with the Haitian flag, just like she wanted it. Even in death, she had the last word. My mother was inconsolable when the men started to lower my grandmother's casket. That was the last we would see her. It had been six days since she passed, but seeing her casket lowered into the ground made it clear that she was finally gone. As Mr. Jean played his gwo ka, he sang a variation of the words inscribed on the casket. *"O swè là sé dzifé nou ka manjé, Jesula sé dzifé ou ké manjé, Jesula ba nou dzifé là, Jesula, sé dzifé aw nou vlé."* Colette Bishara sat with my mother, Junior, and Anouk, consoling my mother as I translated for Zara. "Tonight, we eat the fire, Jesula, you will eat the fire. Jesula, give us the fire, Jesula, we want your fire." Magalie. Clément. Uncle Yves. Pastor Bishara. My father. My grandmother. Eighteen years between the first funeral and my grandmother's. Life being life, we were not done dying or having funerals. I wondered who was next. I should never have wondered such a thought, because either the fire was not done consuming us or the rain was not done falling.

Mehdi didn't come to our home after the funeral, choosing to come the day after, the same day Zara, Eliza, Didier, and Camille returned to Strasbourg on the overnight flight. It had started to rain, and I remember saying to Eliza that when she wakes up again, she would be home and that Uncle Junior, Auntie Anouk, and I would see her in a few days.

"Will it still be raining?" she'd asked. "I don't want it to rain anymore."

"The rain is a blessing. Don't be mad at the rain," Junior had answered.

When Mehdi showed up that evening, the rain had gotten stronger with the wind, and as Junior, my mother, Anouk, and I sat at the kitchen table, we heard him shouting, somewhat incoherently, as if he were intoxicated. As his voice drew nearer, I went to the front door and I was brought back to when Uncle Yves was visiting us that time the sky was falling over Dominica, that time when my father showed up drunk shouting obscenities at my grandmother. It was Mehdi this time, awkwardly making his way up the two short steps to the front door. He barged in past me, soaking wet, swaying, cursing, and smelling of rank goat and liquor.

"I don't know why you have dreadlocks," he said to Junior. "You're no Rasta, you fucking Babylon."

Junior didn't say anything, taken aback by this new situation with Mehdi.

"Mehdi," I said. "How are you showing up here drunk? Let's go! We're not starting no trouble we can't finish tonight."

"Fuck you, Junior! You piece of shit! Fuck you!"

I made a sign to Junior to not say anything and to just let it be.

"You think you're better than me? You nappy-headed motherfucker."

At this point I lifted Mehdi from under his arms, wrapping my hands around his back, and carried him outside. I dragged him in the rain to the passenger side of my rental car. He kept struggling, trying to get free.

"Get in the car, Mehdi!" I said.

When I finally managed to open the car door, I forced him in, shut the door, and leaned against it. As he calmed down, I went to the driver's side and sat next to him. He started pounding the dashboard with his fist in frustration.

"We're gonna work this out, Mehdi," I said. "This isn't the way. Junior is not your enemy."

"There's nothing else to work out," he said. "I'm never gonna be good enough for you all."

Then, all of a sudden, he stopped crying and wiped his face. He became so calm, as if a light bulb had come on in his head, telling him to stop.

"I had a plan to kill him, you know," he said.

"Kill who?"

"Fritzner. I had a plan to kill that asshole. But that Gwada rum beat me to it."

I started the car.

"Junior looks just like that motherfucker. No wonder he hates me. They both do. I swear in that house right now, Fritzner and Junior are the same fucking person."

"Junior is nothing like that drunk."

And then, his face changed. That sweet boy who was buried in that troubled body disappeared. His eyes lost whatever life they had. The interior of the car felt so ominous, I could taste the evil, the hair on the back of my neck rising, myself tense. As he sat next to me, I felt I had come face-to-face with the darkness, as if Lucifer himself had me wrapped in his wings. They were not comforting, just hard bones and scaly cartilage of asthma-inducing distress.

I pushed on the gas pedal, and just as we started moving, he jumped out and rushed back into the house. I slammed the car into park and scrambled to catch up to him, fearing that he would do something vile or that Junior would slam his slight frame on the thinly laminated concrete floor. I found him standing in a face-off with Junior, shaking, he was so angry.

"Why you always treating me like shit?" he demanded.

"I wish you hadn't been drinking and we could actually talk," Junior answered. He was calm and matter-of-fact.

"Answer my fucking question, Fritzner!"

"Take it easy, Mehdi!"

"Fuck you!" said Mehdi as he took a step towards Junior and followed it up with a drunken swing.

Junior sidestepped his weak attempt at a punch in the face and grabbed him as if he were a ten-pound sack of rice. He carried him outside and dropped him just off the edge of the veranda.

"Go the fuck home, Mehdi!" said Junior. "You need to stop drinking."

There was a crack, like the noise made by the end of a whip at carnival. Junior was on the ground with Mehdi standing over him, holding a gun, Junior's outstretched hand pleading for Mehdi not to pull the trigger again.

"Fuck you, Fritzner! I'm tired of you disrespecting me. *Manjé dzifé aw!*"

Mehdi shot him again, four more times. Then, in a moment of clarity, he looked up at us, his face regretful, as if he had finally realised what he had done, that he had killed his own brother, that he had killed his father's child, that he himself was a killer, a murderer, that his half Indian, half Black self was lost and stuck in all the mud from the torrential rain. He was at the mercy of the black, open sky, its belly full with the rage of swelling tides, aimless, like a drifter on a bamboo raft, pillaging his own soul as if it were a demon village on this massive ocean of regret, land nowhere in sight.

He dropped the gun and fled. I could do nothing but watch as one brother ran in the distance and the other one lay there bleeding to death. Mr. Jean's drum was still beating, defiant of the crashing rain, still penetrating the night. The rain engulfed us.

Junior died that night before we even got a chance to call an ambulance. He died at the house that his father built, in front of me, in front of his mother, in front of his wife and their unborn child. Just when we thought we were done crying, the tears came back like a vengeance, knocking us off our feet. This fire that we wanted was nothing next to rain.

Chapter 24

Pointe-à-Pitre, May 2013

We remember our loved ones in parts, in small pieces of themselves—in minute details that bring them back to life. It's in thinking about their smile, their walk, the way they looked at us, their jokes, their talk, their contemplative seriousness. It's in these small things, like catching the short smile of a shy child trying not to, that we remember them. I remembered Junior in all the pieces of him. And as much as those pieces filled me up, they brought me a mountain of sorrow.

On the first-year anniversary of his death, Anouk's mother, Anouk, her new baby daughter Sammy, my mother, Zara, Eliza, and I met in Guadeloupe. We visited Junior's memorial headstone at the Pointe-à-Pitre cemetery. We held hands and offered prayers, words of peace and longing, songs of grace. I wished so much he could have seen his baby, that he could have held her, that he could have treasured the child he loved so much even when she was still in her mother's womb. Not a day went by without me thinking about my brother or feeling like the grief of losing him would ever end. That sorrow was a mountain indeed, a sorrow that could have been avoided, one that never needed to be. It was the kind that laid us flat on our backs. But we got up again after his death, slowly, broken, our faith shattered, our hearts in pieces. We managed to finally breathe deep enough to catch our breath.

We travelled to Dominica a few days later and drove to the countryside hills near the town of Calibishie. I carried Junior's ashes as we walked to the beach.

"I want to do this by myself," Anouk said, handing Sammy to her mother, Awa. I gave her the ashes.

She walked into the water until she was waist-deep, put her bare hands in the urn, and spread the ashes over the water as if she were a flower girl throwing rose petals at a wedding. She repeated this action a few times until there were no ashes left. Then she took the vase, submerged it in the water, and emptied its contents again. She resubmerged it, only this time she lifted it over her head and poured the water over herself, passing her hand over her wet face. She was crying. Like dust to dust, hers were salt to salt, gently at first, and then a full cry, a wailing. We were looking on from the beach, our own eyes no less wet than hers. Seeing her wail, I waded into the water towards her. I grabbed her and steadied her back onto the beach. As we walked out, my mother, Awa, Zara, and Sammy met us. We circled Anouk like prayer around a lit candle as she fell to her knees, sobbing profoundly.

Upon our return to Guadeloupe, only our neighbour, Mr. Jean, came to visit us while we stayed with my mother. It's not that I wanted company, but unlike France, Guadeloupe is a community of drop-ins, where you always make enough food in case somebody drops in at lunch or dinner, where your home is always clean in case somebody stops by uninvited. But nobody came.

There was a stillness in that month of May. I looked out often towards the front door when I would sit at the kitchen table, expecting to see Junior enter. I kept seeing flashes of him, as if my eyes and mind were playing games on me. I could hear him and smell him and sometimes I sensed him, as if he was sitting at the table or under the veranda with me. I felt my brother's spirit.

"I want to see Tatiana," said Anouk.

"She doesn't live there anymore," said my mother. "She and David moved to the country, in Sainte-Rose, closer to their family."

"I need to see that woman. I can't leave this island until I do."

We were silent. Nobody asked her why.

"I saw David a few weeks ago," my mother said. "He told me Tatiana wasn't doing too well. She may not be able to tell you what you need to hear, or even really hear what you have to say."

"Who are these people, Tatiana and David?" Awa asked.

"Mehdi's mother and older brother," Zara replied.

Awa acknowledged Zara's response by raising her chin and clenching her lips, giving a faint nod.

"You know," said my mother, "when Tatiana first started seeing Fritzner, I hated her as much as any woman could hate another woman. Now, well over twenty years later, I don't hate her anymore. I can't even say when I stopped hating her. At some point I forgave her. I can't be sure of when I did that either. But I never told her I forgave her—not to her face anyway. Sometimes I wonder if I should have said something. I feel that she knows I have forgiven her, but I wonder if she truly knows, the same way I wonder if she knows that I know she's sorry without ever telling me."

"I don't know what I want to say to her," said Anouk. "I know she's grieving like the rest of us."

"Yes, she is," said my mother. "She came to see me before she left. I told her not to leave on my account. But she couldn't stay. I feel it was partly for me, but mostly, she could no longer stay in that house."

"Is that where the boy hanged himself?" asked Awa.

My mother nodded.

"Poor child," said Awa.

I didn't know if Awa was referring to Tatiana or Mehdi. But either way, it was a tragedy—Junior's death, Mehdi's suicide, and Tatiana having to cope with it all and relive the trauma of her first husband's hanging.

When Anouk and I got to Tatiana's, it was clear that much had changed for her. She was definitely not the same person who had stood under her veranda, holding her very pregnant belly while telling me I could take my father with me. That Tatiana was long gone. This Tatiana was a shadow of that woman. This Tatiana was just trying to survive. Anouk and I sat at her table, along with her and David.

"We were just in Dominica," I said. "We spread Junior's ashes over the ocean."

"He fell in love with that island," said Anouk. "Well, we both did. It felt right that he rest there."

Tatiana and David did not respond. They looked at us and nodded.

"Tatiana, I remember at Jesula's wake, you asked me when I was due. Do you remember that?"

"I remember you being pregnant and talking about it, yes," she said.

"She's eight months old now. She is named Sammy, after her father," Anouk said.

Tatiana took a second to connect to what was being said, and then smiled. "Yes, Samuel. Fritzner never called him anything but Samuel."

Anouk stared at Tatiana's face, then put her head down, shaking it. "I don't know why I am here, just that I felt compelled to be."

"I am glad to see you. I think of you all often, but I think about you the most, the one I knew the least. I knew you were pregnant, and that child would be born without a father, the one thing Mehdi craved most in the world. My boy wasn't well."

"Well, Widelene's boy didn't deserve to be gunned down like that. Of all the people who deserve such treatment, it wasn't him," Anouk said.

I reached over and grabbed Anouk's hand. She was shaking. The year had done nothing to relieve the pain of Junior's death.

"I'm sorry," said Anouk. "I didn't come here to berate you. Sometimes it's just so hard not to be angry."

"It's all right," said Tatiana.

"My parents are both African," Anouk said. "They moved to France a few years before I was born. And when I was born, my mother wanted to name me Adjoua, because I was born on a Monday. But my father would not have it. He knew how French people were. He didn't want me to stand out and be too different from other children. So he named me as French as you could get. From the very beginning, my father has been there for me."

She started crying through her words. "My father is still there for me. My father loved Junior because he saw Junior's heart. He saw the man he was and the kind of father he would be. I don't know how I can be the type of father Junior would have been to my daughter. She's already starting off at a loss, one that can never be replaced—one that I can't replace."

Anouk's words hit me the same way I'm hit when I realise my brother is no longer there with me. It's realising all that ambition, that dream, that purpose died with him that night, and all that was left was a barrel of emptiness filled with cravings that would never materialise.

"I'm sorry for your loss. I'm sorry for all of you and what you've lost," Tatiana said. "I understand your mourning. I get it. I still, like yourselves, mourn my child. When the police came to my door in the middle of the night, I had no idea what he had done. I didn't even think he was home. I went to check his room and there he was hanging from the wooden beams, soaking wet. I didn't even scream. I had the officers help me cut him down, and then I lay with him on the hard laminate floor. I lay there until the ambulance came. I am so sorry for what he did. I'm sorry he took your husband and your brother from you."

Anouk nodded. Neither of us had heard this part of Mehdi's suicide before. There was strangeness among the four of us. Like David, it was Anouk's turn to be front and centre, only she was not out of place. If Tatiana thought often about her, it was because Tatiana needed the closure that only Anouk could have possibly given her.

"I don't think he was shooting at Junior that night. I feel he was shooting at his father. He was shooting at Fritzner," said Anouk.

She reached across the table and held Tatiana's hands.

"Mehdi shot at his father that night. When he pulled the trigger, that's who he saw in front of him. I know it. I was there. I heard him call Junior by his father's name. We both heard it. In my heart, I don't believe he wanted to kill his brother."

Tatiana was teary-eyed too. She was hanging on tightly to Anouk's hands.

"Fritzner," she said softly.

"Yes, Fritzner."

"May God forgive me."

We had all forgiven Tatiana for the role she'd played in our lives. Whether she understood it or not, that visit was Anouk's way of allaying the guilt and shame Tatiana carried.

On our way home, I stopped at my father's grave site. Anouk stayed in the car. It was hot and I told her I wouldn't be long, but she asked that I take as much time as I needed. As I walked to his grave, I had a feeling of déjà vu, like when I'd last walked to the house he shared with Tatiana, where he poured shot after shot for himself and took long drags of his cigarette. I especially remember the anxious feeling I had in my stomach. And there I was again, no rum, no cigarette, no table under a veranda, just me and a cement slab with a headstone, my father's bones underneath it all.

"I've always wondered if all this started with you. Had you been good to Mom and stayed with her, and not hooked up with Tatiana, not started drinking your rum, would our lives have been better. I wonder all the time, and I can't settle on an answer. It's hard because I wonder if you, yourself, weren't a victim of a demonic cycle, where the best you could do was run, finding women and rum to take away your pain, even for a little while. Maybe we are all running in our own way, and we just don't know it."

I knelt next to his headstone, put my hand on his grave.

"I'm sorry," I said, "that we were not enough to keep you. I don't hate you, I just hate your actions. But none of it matters anymore. I hope you're finally at peace."

I whispered a prayer to him and returned to the car and drove home.

Back at my mother's place we were readying to leave Guadeloupe the following day, and she would come with us. She had no one left in Guadeloupe. She would stay with Zara, Eliza, and me and return whenever she needed. When I told her that I had stopped at my father's grave, she said, "Good. I won't feel bad not stopping at his grave, then." She had the same thought as me, only she wanted to stop at the family plot and talk to her father and mother, her Uncle Yves, and her sister Mirlande. She went there often, but as she was leaving, she wanted to stop by again. Maybe this could have been the last time. When we got there, she spoke to the four of them as if they were there with her, in person.

"Apparently, Africa wasn't big enough for all of us. They had to make some room, so they transported us across the sea to the old Hispaniola, thinking it would be good for us. But even Haiti couldn't hold us. Now Guadeloupe can't keep us either. It's no wonder why we are all so restless, why we can't stay in one place, always moving, going somewhere. If they had just let us be, our spirits could be still. We could find the peace we need."

As she spoke, she cleaned around the graves and headstones, ripping up any weeds near them.

"I pray for you all, all the time. I pray that you have found the peace you need. I know you're all worried about me, about us. But we're all right. I'm moving again, this time with Salomon and his family in Strasbourg, but it's not because I'm restless. There's just nothing else here for me, except for the heat. Over there, I will have two grandchildren to keep me grounded and young. I'll come back and visit whenever I'm on the island. In the meantime, I will tell the little ones everything I can about you. I hope to spend a long time with them, but if I can't, I know where you will be."

She took her time around each grave and kissed each one of the family's headstones before we left.

Back at the house, my mother and I sat for tea one last time at the kitchen table. We looked across at each other. I could see my grandmother in her, not just her mannerisms, but her age—the creases in her face, the veins running through her hands, the grey of her eyelashes.

"I'd give anything," she said, "to sit here and listen to your grandmother tell Junior some nonsense about his third serving of *pwa-wouj-konsomé* or talk to you about Pastor Bishara's sermon as soon as you walked through the door from Lord knows where."

"You've already given everything, Mom. How much more is there in you to give?"

In her answer I realised that my determination to translate the speeches from the Oaths of Strasbourg into Kréyòl had been shortsighted. Our journey had never been in our own hands. Our destiny was never tied to any city—we were brothers, but we were not kings.

"A mother never stops giving," she said. "Even when she's on empty, she'll find something to give. It's the one thing we can never stop doing. If all we could do was sing, we would sing for our children. Child, we would sing like the coucou mayoc before the rain."

ACKNOWLEDGEMENTS

I'd like to acknowledge the following people for their efforts in helping this book come to life:

Lane Clarke, my agent: Your belief in this story encouraged me to believe that it had wings and merited open sky to soar. Chantelle Aimée Osman, my editor: I am still blown away by your excitement for this book, and that our visions aligned so well. I remain in awe that you see so much more beyond the characters. Grace Wynter, my developmental editor: Working with you was seamless. Your input, care, and understanding are appreciated far beyond what words can convey. Philip Pascuzzo, thank you for your vision of a most splendid book cover. Jon Ford, thank you for such detailed and incredibly insightful copyediting. Thank you also to Laura Van der Veer. I appreciate you jumping on at the end and still keeping everything running smoothly, never skipping a beat! To the rest of the Lake Union family, all those who have championed this story, from second reads to publicity, thank you from the bottom of my heart.

On a more personal note, Evelyn C. White, my dear friend and mentor, I will always be grateful for your care, instruction, patience, and laughs. I am proud and thankful for your mentorship in the Alistair MacLeod Mentorship Program. Yes, I believe you when you say to trust in the ancestors. I do, and will continue to do so. Charlene Carr, it is my utmost honour to call you a friend. Thank you for your guidance and patience as you answered my questions—so many questions. Thank you for your incredible support. The Writers' Federation of Nova Scotia, thank you for giving me community. I am proud to be part of such a forward-thinking, inclusive, and convivial organisation. Betty Morgan, I can only hope to be so young in spirit when I am ninety-five. Thank you for reading and believing in my stories. Yasemin and Rosa, you have been superb beta readers. Your unreserved feedback, perspective, and input allowed me to pose questions I most likely would not have, challenging me to take more risks in the development of the story. Thank you for your care. Nancie, thank you for your unwavering support and your belief that it was only a matter of time before the world got to read and appreciate my art. There are no words to adequately convey my gratitude. Roy and Kirk, I am blessed to have friends who tell me the hard truths I need to hear at times. Mom and James, nothing compares in this world to knowing that no matter how far I may be, I can always come home. Thank you for your unreserved encouragement. To all those near and far, in particular Bermuda, Dominica, Guadeloupe, and France, thank you for lifting me.

ABOUT THE AUTHOR

Photo © 2024 Oratile Mogae

Robert de la Chevotière always felt that he had a story to tell, be it through poetry, short stories, song, or fiction. His own story is one of migration. Born in Dominica, he and his mother moved to Guadeloupe shortly after Hurricane David crippled the island. Several years later, they moved to Bermuda. In terms of language, customs, music, food, and socioeconomics, the cultural variation gifted Robert with a cross-cultural understanding of places and people. He now calls Halifax, Nova Scotia, home, where he has been an educator in the public school system for nearly twenty years. To Robert, writing is political, the same way it has been transportive and influential in his own awakening. When not writing, reading, or being a hands-on dad, Robert enjoys video calls with his family scattered around the globe, playing soccer, and enjoying all things of his beloved Arsenal FC. For more information, visit www.robdelabooks.com.